THE

AMACON COVER

Bedside Books
An imprint of American Book Publishing
American Book Publishing
P.O. Box 65624
Salt Lake City, UT 84165
www.american-book.com
Printed in the United States of America on acid-free paper.

The Amacon Cover

Designed by Elles Gianocostas, design@american-book.com

Publisher's Note: *This is a work of fiction. Names, characters, places, and incidents either are the product of the author's imagination, or are used fictitiously, and any resemblance to actual persons, living or dead, events, or locales is entirely coincidental.*

ISBN 1-58982-266-8

Klausman, William J., The Amacon Cover

Special Sales

THE

AMACON COVER

By

William J. Klausman

DEDICATION

This book is dedicated to all those who serve in the United States' and her allies' intelligence services, whose honorable and unselfish achievements are often unrewarded. Their commitment to the security of the United States and her allies protects the freedoms for which I am forever grateful.

FORWARD

Bill Klausman is easy to find. Just Google him and you can read all about his musical talents, his business activities and his public service. But you won't find anything about the Bill Klausman who is one of the most uniquely talented private investigators in America.

I first met Bill some 25 years ago. At that time I had been an investigator for over 20 years, first in the San Francisco Bay Area and then in Portland, Oregon. A new client had given me a major assignment which involved investigating the personal background and activities of various individuals. Since the client demanded the assignment be carried out in the utmost secrecy, with daily meetings to discuss the progress of our work, I knew only one person who could comply with such a rigorous schedule and pull this off. And that was Bill Klausman, or, more correctly, a host of Bill Klausmans operating under a variety of aliases, pseudonyms, and deceptions. The job lasted over 18 months and his graphic reports fill volumes.

Bill's extraordinary abilities as an undercover investigator stem from a broad general knowledge of many places and things and an unusual ability to deal one on one with people from all walks of life. He's as comfortable dealing with a corporate CEO as he is with a doctor, an inventor or marine engineer, all of whom have played roles in his investigative dramas.

As one who has traveled widely throughout the United States and Europe, I have had the privilege of meeting and working with some of the nation's top investigators. The *sine qua non* of a good investigator is the ability to get information. Hal Lipset, the legendary San Francisco private eye, whose career began in the 1940s and spanned 50 years before his death in 1997, was the acknowledged master. Lipset's spacious Victorian home/office in San Francisco's Pacific Heights was the breeding ground for an elite group of San Francisco-based investigators that include David Fechheimer and the renowned husband-and-wife team of Jack Palladino and Sandra Sutherland who stand without peer at the top of the list of this nation's private investigators.

Although these investigators are well known internationally, the work they do in behalf of their powerful and famous clients is conducted outside the public glare of TV cameras and the evening news. These are attributes that Bill Klausman brings to his investigative skills, which are truly unique. He has excellent reporting skills and many times I have been dumbfounded while reading the results of his undercover investigations. How in the world did you get this? I would ask. He would just smile. Sometimes he would recount a strategy that could only have come from the mind of someone who was virtually fearless and with the daring of a burglar.

Alan Crowe

Award winning investigator, lecturer and author

President of Alan H. Crose & Associates, Inc., Mr. Crowe is a renowned legal investigator and process server who authored *Case Investigation* in the Civil Ligitation Manual, published by the Oregon State Bar Committee on Continuing Legal Education. Mr. Crowe was also featured on *Techniques of Legal Investigation* sponsored by Continuing Education Seminars of Clearwater, Florida. He was honored with the *Bert Rosenthal Memorial Award* from the California Association of Professional Process Servers and the *Donald C. Mac MacDonald Award* from the National Association of Professional Process Servers.

PREFACE

Excerpted from "Undercover Inc.," appearing in the
November 1990 edition of *Alaska Airlines Magazine*

"Bill Klausman does not look like a spy as he examines financial statements spread over a desk in the office of a truck dealership. Though his false ID says he's a bank auditor, he is actually snooping around on behalf of his client, an Egyptian trading company that is buying the dealership as a corporate sale—assets and liabilities included. The trading company wants to make sure of its investment, and has a hunch that the seller might be cooking the books. As Klausman sits there, the mail arrives and an IRS window envelope is laid on an adjoining desk. No one is around, so he quickly opens the envelope and reads the Notice of Intent to Lien, for back payroll taxes. He replaces the letter, leaves the office and reports immediately to his client, who rewards him well for the valuable information.

"Tall, freckle-faced and blessed with thick curly hair, Klausman wears a jogging suit and a warm smile. His affable, outgoing personality is one of the reasons he's rarely discovered in his role as an operative in the shadowy world of corporate counter-espionage. If he is detected—and it has happened only once—the result can be the collapse of an expensive set-up, the premature end of a lucrative assignment and a professional embarrassment.

"Spooks, they're called, and nobody knows how many haunt the business world, but sources agree that during the last decade, business espionage has grown tremendously. Corporate spies steal not only secret formulas, but also marketing plans, cost data, and customer lists. Experts estimate that 80 percent of the time the compromised corporation never even realizes it's been hit.

"If a business suspects or knows that vital information has been stolen, it may bring the problem to someone like Klausman. Occasionally, the FBI handles a major case, and some corporations have in-house intelligence departments to deal with information leaks. But more often, businesses turn to outside sources.

"Along with their special skills, these outsiders provide a cushion of deniability. Often, companies want to be able to walk away from the outsider in case something unforeseen goes wrong; thus making it impossible to prove that such a relationship existed.

"Klausman is a specialist in covert counter-intelligence. His targets consist only of those who have harmed, or are about to harm, his clients. Operating alone, he worms his way inside the target organization, gets the proof, and then exits before the target realizes what has happened. He justifies a lot of what he does as the righting of a wrong.

"Although espionage has always existed, the recent upsurge reflects the peculiar conditions in today's marketplace. One factor has been the ethos of wealth and power at any cost that characterizes the job market—job-hopping has replaced corporate loyalty, but even longtime employees have been caught selling secrets.

"Experts agree that the espionage business is fundamentally all about people—how they can be manipulated and what makes them tick. Klausman looks for motivation, and has his own ideas of how and where to find it.

"But most intriguing is his theory about the mirror image. He believes people are so consumed by their foibles that they see ghosts of their own souls everywhere they look. If you want the key to a person's secrets, look at what he says about other people. "When they talk about somebody else, they're really talking about themselves," he says; he has not found an exception to this rule yet."

Klausman's own life provided the inspiration, the experience, and the material for his alter ego, Bill Gale, in *Amacon Cover,* the first in a series of Corporate Espionage thrillers taken directly from Klausman's working files.

*In the original article, a pseudonym was used for
Klausman's protection

ONE

The cargo jet lifted off Kennedy's runway on a routine flight to Frankfurt. The weather was clear and cold. Everything was normal. A quick scan of the instrument panel convinced the captain that the flight would be another routine one. He placed his headset on the outboard console, and turned his head from side to side in an effort to relieve a tension headache that seemed to linger with a nagging head cold.

He rotated his shoulders, stretched his long arms in front of him, and nodded to the copilot. "It's your plane, guy. I'm gonna hit the head."

He uncoiled himself from the controls and stood upright. The captain was relatively tall at a little over six feet two. He made one last scan of the console, then ducked out of the cabin. The two heads are in the tail section, the same as the passenger version of this aircraft. But the similarity ends there.

When converted, the passenger seats were removed, leaving only the aluminum rails—four in all—running front to rear. A dozen or so tie-down rings were attached to the rails to secure the cargo to the deck. Even the decorative trim on the outside bulkheads and overhead luggage compartments were removed. In their place, a grayish, vinyl fabric is the aircraft's only hint of decor—not that attractive, but it covers the raw bulkhead beneath it. Gone, too, are the flight attendants' call buttons, fresh air vents, and reading lamps. This particular aircraft has one mission only—transport extremely secretive and high-dollar cargo. Creature comfort isn't part of the package. Except for an occasional spouse or other friendly hitchhiker, a passenger list is nonexistent. Double bay doors on both sides provide for easy on- and off-loading at any out-of-the-way landing strip. This particular aircraft is custom designed for quick turnaround times.

The captain closed the toilet door behind him and walked forward, straddling the rails, stepping over the tie-downs. He checked each of them for tautness and then placed a hand on the side bulkhead, checking for unusual vibrations. He felt none. He focused his attention on the cargo, a single crate. The night loaders had placed the cargo in the center of the craft to ensure correct weight distribution.

The single crate rested on a wooden pallet. Nothing struck him as being unusual about the crate. At about six feet square, it was a perfect square of tongue-and-groove oak. An expensive crate, the captain thought. A gray canister the size of a coffee can lay secured to the outboard pal-

One

let by two rubber straps whose ends were then secured by a pair of heavy-duty staples. The canister had been placed next to a cardboard box, which had also been secured the same way. The box measured about ten inches across, and the words "SPARE PARTS" had been stenciled in red ink. There were no other markings on the canister. A blue wire poked out of the lid and ran to the box, where it disappeared through a tiny hole. The crate, itself, bore the words "SHIP TO: TRANSCOR FRANKFURT." It, too, was stenciled in red ink. Seeing nothing unusual, the captain returned to the cabin, where he climbed back into the seat and took over the controls.

Four thousand feet below, the ocean's surface was unusually calm. An oceangoing tug glided silently toward the New York harbor; its wake glistening in the early morning sun. The captain brought the aircraft a few degrees to port, continuing its climb. In seconds, the tug was well behind the aircraft. The smoothness of the ocean confirmed earlier weather reports that the northeasterlies weren't due to touch down until late morning.

The captain brought the aircraft a few more degrees to port, straightened her out, and continued climbing when, suddenly, his nostrils flinched at the putrid aroma of bitter almonds. He gasped for breath, then grabbed his throat in a desperate attempt to massage much needed oxygen into his lungs. Instinctively, he forced his tongue out of his trembling mouth to make his air passage larger. He gasped for air as he shoved his fingers in his mouth, frantically probing for an obstruction of any kind, but there was none. His chest muscles expanded and contracted violently as his entire body convulsed, begging for the oxygen it couldn't get. Gasping and sobbing, his head tossed violently backward. He screamed and wheezed as he struggled for air. With a jerk, his head bolted forward and smashed into the wheel. Blood spurted from a hole in his lower lip as his teeth ripped through the flesh. His legs thrashed violently as he jerked his head from side to side until, finally with a relieving silence, his head lay still, blood trickling from his battered mouth.

The copilot had succumbed more quickly. His lifeless body slumped over the controls as the 727 went into a steep power dive. Seconds before impact, a gray canister came to rest against the captain's motionless shoe.

TWO

CARGO JET LOST IN COLD ATLANTIC. NO SURVIVORS

The *New York Times* lay folded on the cushion of the window seat. In the aisle seat, his view of the approaching flight attendant was unobstructed. In his mid forties and well rehearsed at being just about anybody he chose, he gave her a trustworthy smile as she took his empty cup. It clinked like fine china as she placed it inside another cup on the plastic tray.

A pressed, white apron covered her royal blue uniform. Her accent was unmistakably German. "Are you enjoying your flight sir?"

"Ja, thank you. Very Good," he replied in a well rehearsed German accent. He returned her smile. His chosen accent did not match his appearance, and it was for good reason. After today, the confusion would help hinder the flight attendant's ability to recall any part of her brief encounter with the stranger. Putting a name to the face would be impossible, should any law enforcement or government official inquire.

"What is your final destination?" she asked.

"Frankfurt," he replied.

"You have a great flight," the flight attendant said as she turned and walked up the aisle, stopping to chat with the other first-class passengers.

"Danke schoen," he replied, knowing his flight would, indeed, be a good one. And why not? His briefcase was stuffed with unmarked American hundreds, more than last week before his assignment began. Indeed many more!

He caressed an expensive cigar, purchased the day before from a tiny tobacco shop on a busy corner deep in Manhattan's Wall Street district. He tucked it into an inside vest pocket to light up later. He was a small man, the product of a Jewish father and Chinese mother. He carried his father's chiseled features but somehow was blessed with his mother's mysterious eyes. He sported a thin black mustache and, at first glance, appeared to be a timid man, perhaps even shy, an easy hit for a bunch of street thugs. Should they try, their lives of crime would be cut pitifully short.

He traveled alone, and he traveled quickly, all with purpose. He never wasted a step or a gesture, and both were done with perfect timing. His successes were based on results. He got the job done.

Although his range of disguises takes on many identities, the intelligence community knows him simply as Jopaq. He's a hired gun—a paid assassin, a mechanic in great demand by any country or any company willing to step up to the plate and pay his extraordinary fees. His clients swear they've never met him. He's a ghost without a face. His only identifiable trait, if it could be called that, is that he's unidentifiable. People can stare all they want, but it serves them no purpose, for as quickly as he turns away, he's forgotten.

The cabin dimmed, so he switched on the overhead reading lamp. As the last few passengers ambled to their seats, the plane began its final descent. He raised the tray table, then retrieved the *Times* from the empty seat next to him. It was open to the same feature story.

> *...in an interview this morning, the plane's owner, Bortens Air Cargo Service, stated their surprise at the incident and expressed their sympathy to the crew's surviving families. Bortens's attorney, Samuel Rader, said the company would participate in a speedy investigation into the cause of the crash. The Times's investigative staff confirmed earlier Bortens's statement that this was only the second mishap in their forty years of transporting cargo...*

The jumbo jet touched down at midnight on one of the Frankfurt runways and taxied toward the terminal. Yielding to the red running lights of another aircraft, the captain stopped to let it pass, then revved the engines to cross the intersection, heading toward the terminal.

After deplaning, Jopaq followed the crowd of fellow passengers down a one-way hall, through an open doorway under a sign that read, "INTERNATIONAL FLIGHTS— ARRIVING PASSENGERS." He continued down a narrow stairway and through a double doorway, which opened into a large room now filling with arriving passengers.

Inside the bleak room were two sets of counters, the first for passengers with items to declare and the second for those without. Against the wall on the right side of the room were several wooden benches placed end to end, running the length of the wall.

A small tractor entered through one door, towing four trailers piled high with luggage. Two men laboriously unloaded its contents to form a double row of suitcases, travel bags, ski bags, golf bags, and boxes of American souvenirs, neatly arranged in the middle of the large room.

The small, polite gentleman of mixed descent squeezed through the crowd, his eyes searching for one bag. Recognizing a particular soft-sided suitcase, which was wedged between two others, he gently nudged one case to the side, lifted his, and placed it on the floor next to him. Jopaq examined the leather bag to be sure its contents were unmolested. Moving to a position with the crowd blocking the view of the inspectors, he lifted the bag to his waist, removed a small padlock, and placed it into his pants pocket, a trick he'd learned to ward off any nosey inspector enticed by a locked compartment.

He unzipped one of the two side pockets that ran the length of the case. Gently, he inserted two fingers searching for two black nylon tubes. He pulled one partially out, then slid it back inside. He put his arm full length into the pocket and felt down the tubes, searching for breaks. There were none. At the end of the pocket, his fingers found a small box of shorter nylon tubes with caps over their ends.

He held the cap of one between his thumb and forefinger, pried off the cap, felt the moisture of the felt-tip pen inside the tube, and replaced the cap, withdrawing his arm. He closed the pocket while turning the case to examine the other side pocket. Inside of it was a clear plastic bag, which contained pieces of nylon—various sizes and shapes. They, too, were intact, so he zipped up the pocket and let the case drop to arms' length.

With nothing to declare, he chose the counter manned by a face he'd seen many times working the same station. In anticipation, a well-rehearsed story was on the tip of his tongue. The first item to be found by a prying inspector would certainly be a sealed manila envelope full of American purchase orders. As far as the longer tubes were concerned, they were easily described as an unassembled easel for sales-meeting presentations. He was ready to tell a story of how the American capitalists favored the well-engineered German product line over those made in Asia. And, since the Americans bought on emotion, the box of colored magic markers was easily accounted for, so there would be no need to test their strength by tapping them on the metal counter. Only Jopaq knew that beneath the felt tip of each pen was embedded a hollow point bullet. And although designed to detonate only by a firing pin, a sudden blow by a sharp object could prove disruptive. The trigger, firing pin, and other movable parts of the weapon were concealed in the plastic bag. The firing pin was disguised as one of four pins by which the easel would be held together, assisted by a clip that resembled a trigger. Other hardware was similarly disguised.

His West German passport identified him as Heinz Kistler who resided on Wismarer Strasse near Gruneburg Park in downtown Frankfurt. His business cards said he was an auto parts salesman. He could readily describe his marketing of automobile replacement parts and other aftermarket doodads to the German car–driving Americans. If necessary, he could lose them in one of several humdrum tales of American capitalism, knowing the inspectors would not be interested. Once they were lulled into complete boredom, he would simply close his luggage and pass through, unquestioned. He got in line.

"Good Day," Jopaq greeted, carefully placing the soft-sided luggage on the counter. Its metal glides clicked as it touched the stainless surface. "My passport?"

"Yes yes, good," said the officer as he studied the passport. "Very Good, ah, Herr Kistler." He shifted his attention to the suitcase for one last officious look, then returned his eyes to Jopaq. Finally convinced all was in order, the officer closed the passport and returned it, hastily waving the imposter through the gate.

Once again, Jopaq was back inside his homeland without incident. At the curb, he climbed into the back seat of a cab, and instructed the driver to take him to 700 Wismarer Strasse. Lifting the expensive Cuban cigar from his coat pocket, he brought it to his nose and took in the sweet tobacco aroma.

"Please, no smoking sir," the driver said. "Thank you."

Jopaq put the cigar back into his pocket and settled in for an hour's drive to his Frankfurt residence. His latest mission had been accomplished in New York, and he was richer by two hundred thousand American dollars.

Born near Beijing, he remembered little of his ancestry. He spent little time studying his country and his culture because it wasn't important to either of his parents. Most of his childhood was spent with his mother because his father traveled extensively. His studies in Chinese were interrupted every few months as his family moved throughout Asia and the Middle East, for reasons he never understood. When he was a teenager, the family moved to Jerusalem, staying until he was eighteen, at which time they moved again. On that morning, he remembered being awakened by his mother and told to pack his things. A van took the two of them to Iran. Although he should've been confused, he'd moved so many times that this one was just another of many. And, since he'd never received any explanations before, why bother being curious?

Primarily he was home-schooled. His mother seldom tutored him in Chinese cultures. She sometimes included Iranian tidbits she had picked up from history books translated into English, and did what she could to prepare her son for what she thought would be a cold and mostly uncalculated world. He picked up what he could from his mother, but the rest he learned on the streets. As a result of his sporadic education, as a defense mechanism, he withdrew from the societal world around him. He chose, instead, one of fantasy—a clean split from reality.

As an adult, he learned that his father was killed while on an assignment with the Mossad, the Jewish equivalent of the American CIA. The sad thing is that he felt no remorse about it—nothing. For some reason, though, he had the presence of mind to sense that his non-emotions were not normal. While the other kids felt grief, he felt pleasure. The fact that he was so aware of his apathy toward others, and liked it, made him a dangerous asset, sure to be tapped by someone needing such a rare commodity. In every way, he was in absolute control of his life, except maybe for its direction. He knew he had a future but was unsure of how to make it happen. He was fully aware, though, that his life would have purpose.

In the next few years, his inability to consider the feelings of others led him to have no remorse for inflicting pain. He didn't necessarily hate his targets, but only because he couldn't define hatred. It was an emotion for which he had no experience. Oh, the difference between love and hate were real when it involved things—items, possessions, other touchables. He loved good wine. But, then again, he could live without it.

When he reached his midtwenties, a high-ranking officer of Israeli's secret service—the Mossad—got in touch and offered him a job. He wondered if his father's reputation might be the reason for the offer. But no matter, he took it. He and his mother were poor, and, through the Mossad, he escaped from the reality of working a normal job.

In Beirut, a dozen years later, he met his first CIA field agent. Together they infiltrated the Lebanese prison camps, freeing hundreds of hostages. After forming a dependent partnership, each one relying on the moves of the other, they worked as a team for months. It was the closest he ever came to interdependence on another human. But it was, after all, just a job. In the final analysis, the relationship with his partner meant nothing to him. It was the excitement that drove him.

He never accepted the credit for dozens of briefcase bombings of embassies, hotel lobbies, bars, busses, train terminals, and cars. All the while, his employers and his enemies remained nameless and faceless. He had taken so many lives that he couldn't count them. And the fact was, he didn't care. He hesitated only slightly before killing his first victim, a teenage PLO soldier. But he had a job to do. Quickly, he sliced the youngster's throat from ear to ear, leaving him to bleed to death on the bunker steps. From then on, it became routine. He enjoyed killing. He was remorseless in both the planning and its execution. He was good at it. In fact, he was the best. In a short time, he was known as the most deadly weapon in the business. And it was only a short time until the inevitable happened.

The American CIA came calling. As for Jopaq, he was a ready listener. Very quickly, the results he created became the key ingredients that catapulted him into a slot once held by their best shooter. He was a smooth and deadly mechanic—a gifted assassin who easily slipped in, hit the target, and slipped out, ready for his next assignment. His successes grew in numbers until he had finally socked away millions of American dollars in several Swiss, Caymanian, and Bahamian bank accounts.

Jopaq keeps separate residences in Germany, Switzerland, Hong Kong, Jerusalem, and the Dutch Antilles. He knows the countries' customs and languages. He's at home anywhere in the world.

"Stop here please." He instructed the driver to stop in the middle of the block, short of the turn onto Wismarer Strasse.

He gave the usual tip and headed cautiously for the alley. Frankfurt's alleys are like most others in the inner cities of America, with cars parked alongside each other. Most houses have garages, which open onto the alleys. And because it's safer than the streets, kids play in the protected alleys, weather permitting. The major difference between the alleys of Germany and those of America is the amount of clutter. There is none in Frankfurt. No garbage cans to be tipped over by stray animals or prankster teenagers, and no junker cars. The streets and alleys are clean. Every speck of dirt has been painstakingly swept away, a Frau's morning ritual. Jopaq's movements were consistently inconsistent. Depending on his instincts, he might take the sidewalk and enter through the front door, or take the alley and use the garage. Other times, he might enter through the house next door. He owned both, and an underground tunnel connected them.

For now, though, he felt comfortable with the alley. He stepped softly, his rubber heels giving him an added bounce as he quietly made his way down the alley toward the rear entrance. The prewar concrete was old and cracked.

His cautious eyes caught every shadow. He moved left to avoid the bumper poking from under a half-closed garage door and stepped over a grate that, over the half century, had been forced higher than the alley's concrete surface. He could have done it blindfolded.

Two

In the middle of the block, he stepped next to a garage door and stopped, listening for unusual sounds. He looked both ways then quickly unlocked and raised the garage door. He stepped inside, closed the door, and locked it behind him. Hearing no unfamiliar sounds, he continued. Knowing his surroundings, he edged past a late-model BMW sedan to the far end of the garage, where he turned right and moved swiftly down a flight of concrete stairs to a heavy metal door. To outthink a potential intruder, naturally unfamiliar with the layout, Jopaq had installed a rather unusual door with fake hinges on the right; the real ones were mounted inside and on the top so that the door opened upwardly and outwardly, much like a garage door. If an intruder solved the puzzle of the door, it made no difference, for behind it was simply a bomb shelter. He put all his weight against the concrete wall, and it gave way slightly. He pushed harder and a portion of the wall, which had been cut into the foundation, swung open. When closed, the door resembled two expansion joints, which, in the absence of adequate lighting, made it impossible for an intruder to recognize. Inside, a passageway ran underground to the house next door. It was pitch black. At precisely twenty paces, he leaned against another spot in the concrete wall and another door opened.

From upstairs, he felt the pulse from the stereo blaring its rock and roll. Both houses had been outfitted to match his lifestyle. Numerous timers turned on television sets, radios, and lights at pre-selected times, all intending to show outsiders that the home was occupied. Radio and TV volumes were set high enough to provide a reasonable excuse why the hard-of-hearing occupant hadn't heard the door-bell. Phone calls were never a problem simply because there were no phones, only a cell phone.

A rope dangled from the joists above him. Without a speck of light to guide him, he grabbed the rope, which pulled a wooden staircase to the concrete floor. It touched down without a sound. He climbed to the top, and opened a trapdoor leading into a small room. He leaned against one of the side walls, which then rotated on its axis. It led him into a closet adjacent to the master bedroom where the stereo's output was now louder. He flicked on the light switch.

Four wooden shelves were attached to the far wall of the closet. The top one was for his remarkable tools of disguise—hairpieces, eyeglasses, contact lenses and their cases, makeup kits, hair dyes, mustaches, beards, shoulder pads, baseball caps, and hats of all descriptions, including a black American cowboy hat. The second shelf contained other items to alter his identity. The third contained a dozen cameras—automatics, manual, some shaped like fountain pens, cigarette packs, and cigars, and miniatures—recording devices, code scramblers, miniature radio transmitters, and scores of other spying paraphernalia.

His inventory was short on weapons, though. Outside of special contracts requiring custom, high-velocity weaponry, he needed only his bare hands, maybe a handgun with a silencer, or perhaps a razor-sharp blade to perform his occupational tasks. The other walls had racks of clothing hung in perfect rows, spaced evenly to prevent wrinkling, including police uniforms and military uniforms of high-ranking Soviet, German, and American officers, and a priest's robe with a leather strap for concealing an automatic weapon. Typical tourist outfits were arranged by country—an American jogging suit; an Arab's diplomatic three-piece suit with appropriate headgear; a proper British tweed sport coat, ascot, derby, and cane; an Indian's white robe; and a set of Ukrainian festive wear. There was also a nun's habit, several formal gowns, a mink coat, and a woman's purse.

He flicked out the closet light and surveyed the master bedroom. The hall lamp cast a small wedge of light into the bedroom. An array of fictitious family photos hung on one wall. Behind one was an electronic monitor mounted flush inside the wall beneath the frame. Its black light illuminated the white face of his wristwatch, a sign that no window or door had been tampered with during the week that he was gone. Had someone been inside, the black light would've been flashing red.

He opened the small door to a wall-mounted control board and pushed a button to reset the electronics in both houses. A printout squeezed through a tiny slot, its message confirming that all systems were intact and had not been tampered with. So, for now, Jopaq would rest. He'd earned his pay, and tomorrow would certainly be an exciting day.

THREE

The early mid-fall snow blanketed the slopes of Mount Hood with two to four inches of the best powder in the Cascades. As winter took hold, it would be paradise for those who called in sick or skipped school in favor of strutting their stuff on the slopes. As the thrill-seeking hot dogs rode the Palmer Lift from Timberline Lodge to the high glacier, the more cautious stuck to the Mile Run.

A few miles from Timberline, the town of Government Camp lay nestled into the side of the mountain. It was a charming little village, which had grown from a rest stop for wagonloads of settlers on the old Oregon Trail to a thriving winter resort. Within a month or two, the restaurants and taverns would be offering a warm relief from the freezing temperatures outside. A few hundred yards off the main road in both directions, a limited number of mountain cabins sat on leased Forest Service land. Cabins were in much smaller supply than was their demand, driving prices high. Most were vacant during the week, but on the upcoming winter weekends, it will be party time. Kids of all ages will be flocking here, some to ski and some to drink beer, but mostly to pick up on the single life. Every cabin's owner was host to a party on the weekends. Except for one.

A road bearing a dead-end sign branched off from the main road next to the post office. A number of quaint, older log cabins fit in quite appropriately with the more luxurious chalet homes, all hidden among the tall, snow-capped firs as the slippery road wound its way along the mountainside.

At the end of the road, a driveway led to a four-car garage attached to a magnificent cedar chalet. Although not the most expensive on the mountain, it was one of the nicest.

The basement's new soundproofing proved its worth as Bill Gale emptied his Smith & Wesson at the paper silhouette target. The bad guy's head disappeared as six hand-loaded hollow-points found their mark. Satisfied that he still had it, he hung the .357 Magnum on a wooden peg, along with a number of other weapons. He spun the combination dial, closed the floor-to-ceiling double steel doors, and headed upstairs.

Gale collapsed in his favorite recliner. The morning paper on his lap, he sipped on a cold cup of coffee, and stretched his long legs to the coffee table, where he rested his size thirteens. The amber glow of the early morning fire cast a warm spell on the cedar walls. The burning logs crackled inside the stone fireplace, while the aroma of burning alder filled the massive great room, its smoky residue rising through the three-story chimney and escaping into the cold, clear sky.

Gale was great at relaxing. He had to be. His work was taxing, both mentally and physically. He worked hard, and he played hard. And when on assignment, he kept moving. An unplanned stop could cost him time. A sputter could trigger disaster, and he couldn't take the chance. He was a corporate spy, one of the best.

He was six feet two, a little over two hundred pounds, and a double extra large. But, in many ways, he was a gentle giant. His hobbies of weight lifting, handgun shooting, and banjo playing were a rare mixture, but they were also the same talents that worked so well in his profession. As he could perform skillfully in front of an audience, so could he match wits with the target of any assignment. His stage was wherever he chose, whether at a nightclub or at a board meeting. And, he controlled his audience with such skill that they actually believed he was who he said he was. It was no surprise, then, that while romancing a target, he would snatch their secret formula long before they knew it was missing. Truly, he was gifted, yet he used his talents selectively and wisely.

His ability to change identities, sometimes at will, was one of the reasons for his success. Like the chameleon, he could slip into any environment, corporate or otherwise, and under totally believable false pretenses, be welcomed with open arms. To top it off, his exits were so carefully planned that there were never any traces left behind. He was in and out so stealthily that, often, his target would have no recollection of his having been there. In fact, several times he had returned to a scene under different pretenses just to prove he'd never been there before.

His ability to recall and drop names was phenomenal. He had memorized the mistresses, brands of booze, and favorite watering holes of the world's most powerful corporate bosses. He'd been on their yachts, in their villas, and had flown in their corporate jets. He'd been welcomed into their corporate world to talk Beethoven or Bach, fast cars, beautiful women, luxurious yachts, the Mediterranean hot spots and, of course, their need for his special services.

Gale uncoiled his muscular body, grabbed the last alder log, and threw it on the fire. He fetched a refill from the pot on the stove and spread the paper on the counter. Through the window next to the door, the sun's rays hit the trees, casting their shadows on the fresh fallen snow. He placed the mug on the counter as the green light on the fax signaled an incoming message.

The fax read, "Hi BG. 3:00 Pioneer Square. Garage level B. Sam Rader, attorney for Bortens Air Cargo. All checked out and ready to go. Chopper on the way."

He folded the single sheet and tossed it into the fireplace. He lifted the phone's receiver, pressed number eight, then hung up, confirming that the message had been received. He climbed the circular stairway to the master bedroom where he threw his robe on the foot of the bed. He selected navy slacks, a light green sweater, and a tan sport coat and was ready to meet Mr. Rader.

Hearing the chopper's approach, he set the security alarm and went through a door leading to the helipad atop his garage. It took less than half an hour to reach the Pioneer Square Tower, where Gale deplaned and shouted directions to the pilot. "Pick up a Mr. Rader at Flight Center One and bring him here. Give him the directions to level B."

The pilot gave a thumbs-up, revved the engine, hovered at twenty feet, then took off for Portland International Airport.

Gale passed through the yellow railing, down a few steps to the level below the helipad, and through a door leading to a small room and an elevator. He took it to the fifteenth floor, where he unlocked the door to his office. His windows face east, toward the Willamette River. The view was spectacular, its skyline penetrated by newer buildings, each unique in design and modern in structure. The sun was now over Mount Hood and beginning to dry the morning dew, famous in Portland. To the north, Gale marveled at the Mount Saint Helens volcano, a snow cone that had spilled its innards. A block away, Waterfront Park's seawall protected the city from the Willamette's annual spring flood. Joggers were already beginning their daily exercises on the promenade.

The seawall ran the length of the river from the Steel Bridge to Harbor Place, where the shops and restaurants are busy preparing for their daily onslaught of customers. From his office, the entire seawall was visible, and it offered a pleasant visual relief from the daily grind.

Although most offices are not equipped with private baths, his was. The bathroom was stocked with various identity-altering tricks of the trade—mustaches, beards, toupees, glasses, contact lenses, elevator shoes, canes, and even a wheelchair and a leg cast with a hinge for quick deployment.

Gale went to extremes not only to protect his cover, but to protect himself. Even the best screening techniques were no match for a professional. Those pretending to be prospective clients who were, as it turned out, old enemies out to set things straight had burned him several times in his career. So, he met every new client in disguise and in a different manner.

This time he kept it simple and picked the moustache and glasses. Off went the tan coat and on went the coveralls. Rubber-soled work boots to complete the look, and he was in costume. A private key let him into the freight elevator where he punched "PB."

The B level contained a lube rack and a few cans of oil, but otherwise it was simply a parking area. Two banks of fluorescent fixtures provided the light. He'd done such a good job cleaning up after himself last time that the garage was spotless. He wadded up some paper towels just as the elevator door opened, revealing a stylish yuppie-type in a navy business suit.

"Are you BG?" the man asked.

Gale faked cleaning his hands with the paper towels, then extended his hand replying, "I'm BG."

"I'm afraid there's been a mistake—"

"Mistake?" Gale responded. "Aren't you here to pick up your car?"

The wavy, brown hair on the yuppie's head tossed to one side as he shook his head in apparent disgust. "Well, I'll be damned. A wild goose chase."

Gale allowed a few seconds for his instincts to agree with the fax he'd received earlier. He was satisfied that the man in front of him was Sam Rader. "Hold it a second. Are you Sam Rader?"

Rader paused and turned. His high cheekbones were firm and his upper lip quivered for a second as he responded. "You know my name."

Gale walked closer and extended his hand. "I had to be sure. I'm Bill Gale. The man you've hired."

"Wow," he said. "You had me going there."

Gale tossed the wadded towels into a basket then returned a grin. "Enough of this stuff, eh? Let's get out of here." Gale motioned for Sam Rader to follow.

Inside the elevator car, the attorney asked, "Do you really need to be this careful? I assume you've checked me out."

"Mr. Rader. Can I call you Sam?"

"Please do."

"You see, Sam, as corny as it may seem, it works," Gale explained. "For instance, had you been someone other than yourself, you would've been out of here, wondering who I was, and no more the wiser, right?"

"Right," Rader said and nodded in agreement. "Because it worked."

"Sorry 'bout that," Gale said. "What's the next step, assuming that you still wish to hire me?"

"Well, based on your reputation that seems to precede you, I'd say yes," Rader replied. "I realize it's a little quick, but I'd like to continue our briefing in San Francisco. Can you make it?"

"If the flight's open," Gale replied. "I can make it by midmorning."

"I'll explain everything there. And you might pack for a few days too," Rader urged.

The elevator door opened into a concrete hallway that led to the roof. Even at idle, the chopper blades spun the dust through the hallway like a wind tunnel. As the two men crouched at the chopper's starboard door, Gale patted Sam's shoulder. "I'll see you in your office tomorrow morning."

As Rader cinched his shoulder harness and nodded his approval, Gale closed the chopper's door. The chopper's blades revved higher as it lifted off the pad and headed back to Portland International Airport. Gale had chartered this craft from an old friend who had served with him in the sheriff's office back in the sixties.

Gale received many assignments in the same manner, through a retired deputy who studied law during his time off. He never passed the bar but knew more about criminal law than most members. Now a private eye, Alan Crowe had gained some notoriety as good investigator. By mutual agreement, Alan screens all Gale's calls, which originate from an ad in the *Wall Street Journal* After running a level-one check, mostly background and employment data, Alan sends a fax, explaining the details, including the time and place for the first meeting. After that, level two is up to Gale. He trusted Alan as much as he did his old buddy, the pilot, and kept their identities and his relationship with them secret from everyone.

Three

As far as clients were concerned, he always used a similar method for their first meeting. Unlike the case with Sam Rader in which a second meeting was necessary, most clients are never seen after the first meeting. Instead, Gale relied on the phone, fax, or e-mail to report his progress and receive client inputs. His clients preferred the anonymity in case something went wrong. And it sometimes did, especially if the target became overzealous to the point of accusing his clients of hiring an unethical PI, who used any means available to get the job done, even if a few laws were broken. Gale would never be identified in court or, heaven forbid, a lineup.

There was no way to reach Gale other than through Alan. His payments for services rendered came by wire transfer into an account that bore a fictitious name. He covered his tracks well and cautiously. True, Bill Gale was a fictitious name to begin with, but he'd still used caution in dealing with Sam Rader, especially to maintain his anonymity. When the assignment was completed, Rader's only knowledge of him would be his physical appearance, a few details gleaned from their meetings, and an untraceable phone number.

* * * * * * *

In San Francisco, Market Street was teeming with activity. The yellow cab swerved to avoid an aggressive jaywalker, then pulled to the curb between intersections. The cab made the trip from United Airline's terminal to the edge of San Francisco's financial district in just under forty minutes. He paid the driver and walked the last few blocks along Market, headed for Montgomery Street.

It was a refreshing change from his quieter hometown streets of Portland. Two electric buses passed within inches of each other, sparks falling like a welder's trail as the spring-loaded carriage skipped over the high-voltage wires. Pedestrians and vehicles alike yielded as the buses headed for their next stops. At every corner, city-bound commuters hopped off and crossed against the lights, attempting to reach their destinations.

Market Street had changed over the years, but the city was still the city. Most of the storefronts were different now, and Nordstrom was a new addition. As he crossed Market in front of a city bus, he recognized the corner tobacco shop. Except for a fresh coat of paint, it was the same.

"How ya doin'?" He picked up a fresh *Examiner* and handed the old man a dollar. Gale took in a deep breath of fresh morning air, and welcomed the scent of the city's familiar sea breeze and salty air as it blew gently from the bay. It brought back fond memories of weekends spent here while attending Stanford Law School in nearby Palo Alto. He smiled as he visualized throttling up California Street in a black Triumph TR3.

Back then, the biggest decision he had was what to do with a law degree from Stanford since, like his PI buddy Alan, he was unable to pass the bar. So, he moved home to Portland and became a cop. After a few years on the streets, he took a look at the CIA. He thought it was a natural move. After all, he loved adventure and it would be an exciting chapter in his life. Gale matured in their intense training program, but living in extreme-cover conditions bothered him. Not even his family knew where he worked, and unlike his present business, he had no control over his life, especially whether he'd make it through any given assignment or not. Disillusioned, he withdrew from the "Company" and headed home.

But, he must have impressed someone in Langley. After a few months, he had received a call from a former instructor, who was now a high-ranking senator in Washington, DC. The senator explained that he'd been in contact with a high-ranking corporate executive needing someone with Gale's talents to do for private industry what he had been trained to do for the Company—infiltrate the enemy camp and get information, Gale supposed.

Honored by the compliment and eager to get started, he had made the contact and begun an exciting twenty-some years in business espionage as a counterintelligence operative. Gale never got the chance to thank the senator for the lead. He was still learning about the nasty business of intelligence gathering at the corporate level because it seemed as though each assignment was a new experience and brought on challenges he'd never met before. What he'd learned of the martial arts had stayed with him to some degree, but he admitted that he was more at home on the Nautilus machines than on the Kung Fu mats. He retained his expertise in the art of point shooting and could, without aiming, hit a fast-moving target with alarming accuracy. Often, these skills helped him resolve certain business problems on behalf of his clients. With the big dollars at stake, he'd learned that some corporations played their secretive games with as much tenacity as the government.

Trade secrets and other illegal commodities, including controlled substances, were bought and sold like common stock. A few less buyers perhaps, but nonetheless highly negotiated, very liquid, and very expensive.

A block off Market Street, the offices of Bortens were in the Commonwealth Building on Montgomery Street. He grasped the brass handle of the massive glass door and stepped from the hallway into the gracious foyer. The decor spelled money. The carpet was a luxurious dark green and felt soft under his step. The small evergreen trees in oak containers made a natural forested boundary from the foyer to the hallway, leading to what Gale anticipated were equally fashionable offices for Bortens's staff. In the middle was a circular desk topped with a marble counter.

Behind it sat a lady in her midtwenties. She sat straight, her silk blouse buttoned at the neck. As Gale entered, she was on the phone saying, "Mr. Rader is with a client. May I ask him to return your call? Yes, Mr. Albrecht. I'll tell him."

She looked up from her console and noticed Gale. "I'm sorry. It's been like this all morning."

"No problem," Gale replied. "Bill Gale to see Sam Rader."

"Mr. Rader is expecting you. I'll let him know you're here." She gave him an appraising look and said, "Please have a seat Mr. Gale."

Within minutes, Sam Rader had stepped into the foyer. "Bill. Nice to see you. How was your flight?" he asked, escorting Gale to the corner office.

"The flight was good. Thank you."

Sam Rader's tenth floor office was tucked away in a plush corner of the Bortens home office. Against one wall were two oak planters containing bushy green plants. On the wall, two frames held certificates of achievement. One was a doctorate of jurisprudence from Harvard School of Law and the other a certificate of current membership in the California State Bar Association. Three separate windows ran from the top to the bottom of the opposite wall overlooking Montgomery Street and the financial district. Rader stood before it and motioned for Gale to take one of the leather chairs in front of the desk.

"By the way, you look different this morning. The coveralls and, of course, the grease were good touches." Rader smiled.

"Sorry about that," Gale responded. "It's nice to be back in the city. I've always enjoyed it."

"Well, I'm glad." Rader leaned back in his chair and opened the file folder. He smiled and asked, "Shall we get into it?" Gale nodded, sat back, and listened.

"Let me start at the beginning. Bortens Air Cargo Company owns a plane that crashed off the coast of New York."

"That's pretty serious!" Gale exclaimed. "What was the cause?"

"I'll get to that in a second," Rader replied. "As you probably have guessed by now, our corporate offices are here in San Francisco. Although our flight headquarters are at Los Angeles International, on the opposite side of the field from the main terminal, our stockholders live in the Bay Area, so it follows that this is home. We're not the largest cargo company by any stretch of the imagination, but to those in certain circles, we are the most prestigious.

"Circles?" Gale asked.

"Let me stall you on that one too," Rader replied. "Our fleet contains the latest aircraft—some built by Boeing, some by Douglas. For this reason, plus the fact that we hire only the most seasoned pilots, our safety record is unbeatable. Along with that particular aircraft, our fleet numbers twenty—nineteen now—a mixture of 727s, 747s, DC-10s, and a couple of well-outfitted attack choppers, which are maintained at the ready—fueled and standing at parade rest. Half the fleet flies out of Kennedy in Washington and the remainder out of Los Angeles. Our customers number only a few."

"Like?" Gale interrupted.

"Select branches of the U.S. Government," Rader explained. "That's it!"

"I see."

"This aircraft flew out of Kennedy. Most of its hours were spent flying in and out of tiny airstrips in Iran, Iraq, Saudi Arabia, Lebanon, Egypt, and other lesser-known places in the Mediterranean, plus a few in Eastern Europe. The aircraft of our Los Angeles location hit the Far East."

"Fairly select audience, I'd say."

"By rather unique design," said Rader. "OK, here's what's happened so far. The plane that went down out of Kennedy?"

Three

"Yes."

"It was a little unusual."

"How do you mean?" Gale asked, as he slumped into the soft leather chair.

"The circumstances surrounding it."

The soft-spoken attorney stood and removed a tailored, dark brown suit coat, gently placing it over the arm of the vacant chair. He tugged at the cuffs of his blue button-down shirt and returned to his chair.

"Circumstances, you say. Like what?" asked Gale.

"Like, for instance, there was no distress call broadcast. I assumed there were vessels out there. After all, it's right in the shipping lanes heading in and out of the biggest harbor on the Atlantic. Other than a tugboat crew, nobody saw or heard anything. I mean, the plane just vanished! Without a sound."

"What was she carrying?" Gale asked.

Rader hesitated, then answered, "Well, the cargo's not important."

"Why do you say that?" Gale asked.

"It's just that we take very good care of our aircraft."

"So what are you saying?" Gale asked.

"What do you know about Bortens?" asked Rader.

Gale leaned forward and replied, "I know you're smaller than Federal Express."

Rader rested his elbows on the desktop and attacked a paper clip, prying open its curves, making it perfectly straight. "You're right about that. We're small globally, but we're quite important." He threw the straightened paper clip into the empty wastebasket. "We haul a considerable amount of freight on government contracts."

"What sort?" asked Gale.

"Let's say one of NASA's prime contractors wanted to buy a hydraulic rocket positioning system for the Cape."

"From a private contractor?" asked Gale

"In this example, let's say yes. We'd make the delivery."

Gale remembered scanning the article in the *Oregonian* while on the plane this morning. "The paper mentioned Iran. I suppose you fly there?"

"Yes. Medical supplies mostly." The alert, clean-shaven attorney could smell the next question a mile away. His smile was timed perfectly to Gale's question.

"To the contras?"

"Something like that." Rader's smile broadened.

"And weapons?" Knowing he'd hit a sensitive tooth, Gale backed off. "So what about this particular shipment?"

Rader pinched the bridge of his nose as if the stress of keeping information from his newly contracted and very perceptive investigator was quite enough for one morning. Not quite a migraine in formation, but enough that he'd better level with the investigator if he was to expect results. "Many times, we're unaware of our cargo's contents."

Gale leaned back in the chair. His legs straight out before him, he placed one shoe on top of the other. Fingers interlocked, he placed his hands on the back of his head, pressing against his curly hair. A smile formed on his tanned face. Blinking to center his contacts, he formulated another question for the Bortens in-house attorney.

"So, let's talk about the cargo. Is there any reason anyone would want the cargo buried at sea?"

"I can't imagine," Rader replied sincerely.

"What was it?"

"A satellite tracking system."

"Can you be more specific?" asked Gale.

Rader referred to the file folder, turning a page over. "A defensive system to track incoming missiles."

"You're talking missiles, like we know them—surface to air, air to surface? From where?"

"Anywhere," Rader replied, hoping his answer satisfied the investigator. "The broker in the deal was Transcor Corporation. They're in Germany—Frankfurt to be exact. Ah, let's see. The seller was Turner Engineering. They're in New York City and in Washington as well."

"Washington?" Gale asked in surprise. "Why there?"

"They're the manufacturer," replied Rader.

"I see. So what's our goal here?" Gale asked, still very much in the dark.

"It's a bit complicated. I think the best way for you to get into it is to accompany me to New York for our FAA hearing. Did you pack enough?"

"I'm good for a week," Gale replied.

"Good. We'll do the FAA hearing first. Then we have a court date set for two days after the hearing. Also, in New York. In fact, I was about to return a call to FAA's attorney when you arrived."

"Court? Could you explain?"

"It's routine, sort of. The crew's families have hired an attorney to represent them. Dieter Albrecht is his name. It seems they now want a bit more than what our contract provides."

Gale stood and stretched his legs, as he remembered the receptionist's phone conversation. He walked around the chair, scanning the two framed documents. "Not a bad school, Harvard," Gale mumbled, and turned to face Rader. "How much are they asking for?"

"Ten million." Sam replied.

"Ten million?" Gale echoed.

"It's a lot, but we're not too concerned that they're aiming high. Well, except maybe for Albrecht."

"So who is Albrecht?"

"A bad ass lawyer from the East Coast."

"How bad?"

"Bad. He's been linked to Washington, politics and all." Sam raised both eyebrows and checked his watch. "It's nearly noon. How about lunch?"

"If you don't mind, maybe we can grab a bite later." Gale made a mental note to learn more about Albrecht as he walked to the credenza and poured two cups of coffee. He handed one to Rader, then sat back into the leather chair, holding the cup with both hands.

As Gale did this, Rader continued his story, "Bortens is owned by three shareholders, all of whom were in the freight-forwarding business way back when. We're not listed anywhere, and originally it began, kind of, as a fluke. Years ago, our owners were being gouged by shipping companies because their shipments, individually, were small. Collectively they could combine their cargo and cut costs if they shipped to the same destination. All they had to do was package the goods and deliver to the docks. It worked out OK for a while, but soon the shipping companies raised their rates."

Gale sipped his coffee. "It must've been long ago?"

"It was." Rader took a small drink of the black coffee, then continued. "Somehow they all got together and decided with the increasing value of their cargoes, they could buy their own airplane and ship their goods themselves."

"Didn't their shipments increase in size along with increased values? I mean individually?" Gale asked. "And why their own planes?"

"Good question. You see, the owners wanted their own planes so they could fly to out-of-the-way places and—"

"And not be detected?" Gale interrupted.

"You're getting warmer."

"So, let me guess. You're hauling contraband," Gale said. "So why did the plane go down?"

"This is what I can tell you," Rader said. "In fact, it's all that I know. The equipment that was lost at sea was very expensive and highly secretive. As you know, our government is very active in Germany. And although there are some who would argue that our usefulness is long outlived, still the USA is there to stay. You can see why. We're right in the middle of it all. With the tearing down of the wall and the wearing away of the USSR and its economies, we've got to stay and protect our investments. So, we do our part and ship things in and out of there nearly every day."

"OK."

"I have a ton of things to do," Rader said. "Let's pack it in for now."

As the two men made their way to the street floor, Gale mentally replayed Rader's comments, and knew there was much more to learn if he was to have any chance of getting up to speed and doing Bortens any good. He had lots of questions needing answers but, as of yet, lacked a basis for formulating them.

Stepping onto the sidewalk, Rader turned to face Gale, extending his hand. "If you'd care to do some sightseeing, feel free," Sam urged. "Tomorrow will be a busy one. I'll pick you up first thing in the morning."

When Gale returned to his hotel room, he made a quick call. "Senator Kent Brewer? Bill Gale. Still kicking?"

"It's been a while, and yes, I'm still kicking."

"What do you know about Bortens Air Cargo?" Gale asked. "Ever hear of them?"

"Why do you ask?"

"I've been asked by Bortens to look into a plane crash carrying a certain cargo."

"Do you know about it?" asked the senator.

"I know it must be important because of all the hullaba-loo," Gale replied. "Is it?"

"I'm not in the circle anymore, as you can probably guess. This legislating business keeps me busy full time. But, as I taught you, be damned careful and keep your head down because they're shooting live ones out here."

"You mean in general?" asked Gale.

"Pretty much so," the senator replied. "If you use your usual instincts, you'll probably learn that like anything involving government contracts, this particular situation is something more than a simple plane crash. Maybe a lot more, who knows!"

"Can you give me a for-instance?" Gale asked again.

"Not really," the senator continued. "Basically, I'm out of the loop and have been for years. I do know, though, that Bortens is clean, but I can't say the same for whoever hires 'em. The streets of DC are soiled with dirty deals. I taught you that in the Company classrooms. Remember?"

"How well I do."

"Well then, remember to cover yourself at all times. As I said, I wouldn't doubt that there'd be more at stake than the cargo sitting at the bottom of the sea. Got to go, and remember, keep your head down."

The dial tone drowned out Gale's next question before he could ask it. Cradling the handset, he replayed Senator Brewer's warnings over and over, hoping for a clue. Surely there was one in what he said, but nothing stood out, at least not yet.

* * * * * * *

The next morning, Gale and Rader caught the red-eye to New York City. They grabbed a cab, sped across the Brooklyn Bridge, and took a right onto Manhattan Island. Gale studied the area briefly because he knew he'd stick around after Rader flew home. Three blocks later on the left, they stepped onto the sidewalk in front of the ten-story federal office building. The marble building looked and smelled like government. It was across the street and down a few blocks from the State Office Building. Running the length of the block, its white marble steps were typically spotless.

"This place is definitely ornate," Gale commented sarcastically, as both men entered the elevator. Rader pushed floor eight, and the elevator's door closed. It opened at the offices of the Federal Aviation Administration, room 818. A male receptionist, dressed in a wrinkled white shirt and speckled bow tie, greeted them and, while pointing to a barren but brightly lit room in the corner of the eighth floor, he beckoned them to find their own way.

Although the door had no identification, Gale guessed that it was their one and only conference room. In the center of the elongated room sat two massive antique oak tables. On each side and at the end were matching chairs whose high backs curved down to become armrests. Bare white walls were the only backdrops, which added absolutely nothing to the flavor of the place.

"Nice place," Gale commented.

As Rader nodded, the door on the opposite end of the room opened and a short, balding man entered the room and took his place at the far end of the first table. He was sporting a button-down shirt and a brown bow tie that matched a dingy pair of tan polyester trousers. Although every bit officious, a thin wire-rimmed pair of spectacles gave him away as a wannabe Village person.

"Good day, gentlemen. My name is Dale Wilson, inspector for this particular case. First, I want to thank you for coming." He placed a stack of manila file folders on the table and waved Gale and Rader to have a seat. "Let's see now. You must be Sam Rader." Turning to Gale, he asked, "And you are?"

"Bill Gale." He replied flatly, giving no reason for his attendance. No one offered, and no one shook hands.

Gale and Rader took the two seats across the table from Wilson.

Wilson sat down, began flipping through the files, looked up at the two men across from him, and said, "Well, gentlemen, what I have here are dossiers on Captain John Avery and Copilot John Whitmore." He continued turning the pages, describing their contents as he flipped each one over. "Blueprints, drawings, photographs of the aircraft—some taken when new, some more recent, log books since the day it was put into service, maintenance records supplied by your New York office, inspection dates, a statement from the deckhand of the *Pisquale*—the tug on the scene when the aircraft went down—and the reports written by our investigators."

He closed the files and rearranged them in the right order from top to bottom, then looked up. "That's about it."

"Any debris?" asked Rader.

"Unfortunately, gentlemen, nothing from the aircraft is available."

"The site. Have you determined the site? Where it crashed?" asked Rader.

"Yes. A few miles offshore. Beyond the shelf. I'm afraid it's in deep water, gentlemen."

"And the cause of the crash. Have you determined the cause?"

"Our theory is this, Mr. Rader. The only witness was the chap on the *Pisquale* tug. His statement verified the engines were at full throttle. From a layman's point of view, it appeared that the pilot flew it into the ocean on purpose. A nose dive."

"Don't you find that a bit odd?" asked Gale.

The inspector ignored Gale's question and, instead, addressed Rader. "We have no reason to believe it was anything but pilot error." Wilson stood, picked up his files, and slid his chair under the table. "If there's nothing more, gentlemen."

"Mr. Wilson, please." Rader stood and demanded more answers. "This is it? The hearing? You're telling me this is it? Pilot error, period?"

Wilson supported the files on his right hip with one arm while the other he extended, palm up, shrugging his shoulders. He stood firm. "Please understand, Mr. Rader, there isn't a speck of evidence, only testimony. And that testimony, I'm afraid, is from one person. I'm terribly sorry I couldn't offer you more. You may wish to talk to your salvage people." He turned and was in the middle of the exit doorway when he stopped and turned around to face them, again expressing his apologies.

"I'm sorry. Truly sorry." He left them staring at each other.

Rader's face had turned red with anger. "That son of a bitch just kissed off this case, big as hell. I don't know who he is or what's going on, but you just don't proclaim a plane's gone down and maybe it's due to pilot error without a full investigation. That's a crock!"

Gale put his hand on the attorney's shoulder and shook his head in full agreement. "Let's get out of here."

Outside on the marble steps, Gale admitted to him, "Sam, I've never been involved in a plane crash, so I'm afraid I'm not up on the lingo. But I can tell you this. The cagey little bastard knew more than he was telling."

"I thought so, too." Rader checked his watch. "Hey, I've got a five o'clock flight back home. Why don't I call you tomorrow night at your hotel? In the meantime, why don't you look around and call me if you find anything." He wrote a number on the back of a business card. "Here's my home phone." Rader caught the first cab to the airport.

* * * * * * * *

Although the lobby was busy, the hotel bar, which was just off the lobby, was quiet. The low lights gave the red, black, and white flowered wallpaper a speakeasy atmosphere out of the thirties. The bartender was dressed to match with long, white sleeves supported by red garters and a handlebar mustache that jiggled as he talked. In red letters, his white name tag spelled "NICK." Running the plastic sword through three olives, he dropped the pimento out of one and placed them inside the steep-sided martini glass filled to its brim with gin. He placed it on the bar in front of Gale.

Gale selected a table in the corner and took a sip of the martini, swirling the olive then eating it. He mulled over the statements made by the FAA official, suggesting pilot error as the probable cause. Although he knew nothing more about Bortens other than what he'd learned in a few hours from Bortens's attorney, his hunches about them were good, and he believed they were efficient at flying their planes. He knew also that their safety record was nearly spotless.

He replayed his meeting with Sam Rader and what he had learned and not learned about the Bortens organization. Barely the tip of the iceberg, he figured. And Wilson, the FAA stooge? He had to be covering up something, but what? And why?

FOUR

The 120 Loop is an old but heavily used highway. Beginning a few miles south of the CIA's Langley campus, adjacent to the Potomac, it winds its way through the picturesque Virginia countryside, through the western suburbs of Arlington, past the Arlington Hospital, and finally catches the Potomac River just above Alexandria. It used to be that the Company's more aggressive drivers accelerated down the loop, heading for home after a long day of interpreting photos, studying radio transmissions, or performing any other items of trickery assigned to them. Now, though, it's more heavily traveled, and, while still a shorter route home, speeds are more in line with the posted speed limits, at least when the radar guns are out.

The Arlington Racquet Club is about halfway between Arlington and Alexandria. On twenty acres of old growth timber, about a hundred yards off the loop on Arlington Boulevard, it's right in the middle of everything, a quick drive to any number of quaint shopping areas and, more importantly, to many government-permeated leisure sites.

Fifty years ago, a high-bidding government contractor was awarded the job of building the new club. Rustic for its day, its flavor of the seventeen hundreds permeates its outer shell, through which entry can only be accessed by a chosen few. Although its founders had intended it to be a gathering place for the rich, that concept had evolved into the current membership roster. While its reputation lingered as an exclusive club of snobs, catering to tennis, racquetball, and off-track betting, it was in reality the official hangout for Washington's power brokers. Although money wasn't necessarily the measure of membership, power, and what it brought in terms of connections, was. Even to be admitted as a guest, one needed to be connected. A few members made modest livings by arranging trips for some of the lesser-known, but nonetheless more powerful, congressmen. Others reached their clandestine objectives through careful negotiations with foreign heads of state. Arms deals were made here at the clink of a cocktail glass.

It was a remarkable setting. Powerful players in the international marketplace brokered deals that changed the lives of American citizens and those abroad. Very serious and very expensive deals were cut on the tennis courts and in the bars. The club housed black-market politics and worse.

Although difficult to penetrate as an aspiring player, those who either earned or bought their way in became quickly and deeply entrenched in its bucket line, passing goods, services, and information to and fro. And their reward? Sometimes wads of cash but, mostly, returned favors. They made their nightly appearances here and, yes, the press would have killed to get inside.

Limousines, mostly Cads and Lincolns, were parked in neat rows in the lot, overseen by a handful of valets, well trained at spotting intruders, especially the press. Overhead halogens cast a bright bluish light over the fleet and, other than a whitewall or two, all limos were basically the same. They were detailed in direct proportion to the size of their passengers' fiscal budgets.

Now and then a classic Mercedes or Jag roadster pulled into the valet parking area. The only covered area on the grounds, it was reserved for a select clientele, mostly power brokers.

The place was crawling with men in black suits and dark shades. They lurked about the facilities but remained, for the most part, unseen once their employers were safely inside. It was their duty to monitor who entered and who departed, and should someone attempt to enter without proper authority, the intruder would be swiftly escorted away.

Although the president and cabinet members rarely showed their faces, many of their associates did. Included were congressmen and senators who may have been invited to share an idea or two proposed by various lobbyists and other special interest leaders. Mostly though, at any given time, the bar was frequented by those who had the deepest pockets and the most power in the world, including prime ministers, kings, premiers, heads of states, and anyone else answering to "your highness." All had connections, and were eager to barter something they had for something they wanted.

The grounds were manicured. The path leading from the parking area to the main entrance was paved with used brick, which had settled into a sea of green moss. Fingers of old-growth ivy wound up and around the leaded glass windows, covering the brick walls with a sea of variegated shades of green.

Surrounded by a twelve-foot-high brick wall, several outside tennis courts were inactive this time of year. Wind-blown oak leaves were scattered about the far end of the courts, resting until the next big blow. Some of the court surfaces were of rubberized asphalt, but most were professionally prepared grass. Top players from around the world would have loved to play here, but only a select few were invited, mostly at the whim of management. During the summer months, the outside courts had long waiting lines. But these days, with the play more intermittent, most chose the inside courts.

"Set point!" The prince's follow-through was graceful. The fuzzy, yellow ball squeaked as it hit the surface beyond the white line.

"Long," answered his tall, slender opponent. "One more, your highness." Confident in the other's advanced prowess and thirsty for a cocktail, the commoner planted his Nikes firm against the rubber surface. He swayed left to right, anticipating the swift serve. He was no match. Resolved to lose, a crooked smile formed as he nodded that he was ready. "Serve the damn thing!"

The Saudi prince threw the ball straight up and, with the finesse of a pro, brought the racquet down with a calculated motion. He struck the ball softly and precisely. It lofted high and slow. It skimmed the net and hit the court's surface, barely a foot inside his opponent's court, then took a tricky bounce out of bounds. It hit the side wall and bounced toward center court. A master at control, the prince planned his serve much as he planned his life—one step ahead of his opponent's.

At first, the commoner in Nikes just stood there, hands on his hips, racquet pointing down. He shook his head and grinned. The game was over, and he was glad.

"A little English spin, perhaps?" laughed the prince.

The two met at the net and shook hands. The prince placed his arm around the shoulder of his losing opponent as the two headed briskly to the side bench with the net between them. Joking, the loser grabbed two towels from the bench and threw one at the prince, who caught it with the tip of his racquet. Long-standing opponents, they were both members in good standing of Washington's elite set. Swinging a yellow sweater over the shoulder of a sweaty polo shirt, the prince escorted his opponent through a door and into a carpeted hallway leading upstairs to the club's private lounge.

This lounge was the only place to rendezvous. And as such, it offered a safe haven for secret meetings of every kind. More often than not, major decisions of global importance were engineered during match play and finalized over a drink.

"Loser buys!" joked the prince. The damp towel made a high-pitched crack as it narrowly missed his opponent's thigh.

His opponent swerved to avoid it, then sat in a leather chair next to a round cocktail table. "Your ass buys!"

The buyer of the first round, indeed, would be Prince Abdul Anini, second in command of the Saudi government. With a doctorate in mechanical engineering from Dartmouth, the very shrewd brother of King Saud was a powerful player in Washington. Other than his unmanageable long and oily black hair, especially after a tennis match, his appearance was still nearly flawless. His clothes were fresh from London's finest boutiques. He had the money to spend, and he wasted no time spreading it around. His family boasted of their successes throughout the world, especially in America.

With the king's blessing, the prince had established a family office in Washington for several reasons. From here, he managed his family's American investments, which included huge chunks of commercial real estate, namely four square blocks in downtown Manhattan. The family's petroleum interests were a guarded resource, and because of them, he chose his associates very carefully. America was a strong ally and a valued reference to the world's oil buyers and, of course, a good friend to the Saudis. He also enjoyed impressing others as he powered a Formula One car around the track.

Accepting the prince's first round was a gracious Daniel Seward. President of Transcor Corporation, an international trading company with offices in Washington, New York, and Frankfurt, he had retired some ten years ago from the Army. His last command was as the liaison officer to Saudi Arabia. In those times, he had resided and worked at the American Embassy where it was fairly easy, and most often a pleasant chore, to keep a watchful eye on the Saudi oil fields. During these years, he met the prince and his older brother, the king. It was from this relationship that prosperous ventures sprang up, providing Seward with healthy profits as a side benefit.

Seward's otherwise fair skin was tanned by numerous visits to the Mediterranean. His broad shoulders and athletic appearance was proof that he was a real mover. He was a handsome man, and being cool wasn't something he found necessary to practice. Through his innocent eyes peered a surprisingly ruthless businessman who would stop at nothing to make a buck, or a million. The stakes in the games he played were always high enough to add credence to the old adage that if you can't afford to lose, you can't afford to play.

The waiter politely served their gin and tonics and briskly walked to the next table. Prince Anini took a deep breath and let his athletic shoulders relax. "Well, my friend. What's next?"

Seward held the tall glass in both hands and gently wiped the frost from the glass. He ran his fingers through a full head of dark, wavy hair and looked at his old friend and business associate. "I'm not sure at this point."

Prince Anini scowled. "You're making me nervous, Daniel. Can it be recovered?" He took another sip, then placed the tall glass on the paper coaster.

"We're looking into it. It's down pretty deep."

"But Daniel, you Americans invented the sport of deep sea diving."

"I Know Abdul. But, There May Be Another Way." He Blotted The Last Remaining Beads Of Perspiration With A Fresh Napkin, Then Folded The Napkin And Placed It Next To An Empty Water Glass.

"Ah, But We Have Already Paid A Large Sum. Up Front. We Want The Merchandise. You Can Do It Daniel." He Lifted His Glass And Took Another Sip.

"I Know. Believe Me, I Understand." Seward Frowned. "I've Been In Contact With The Supplier. I Think We Can Purchase Another One—"

"Daniel," The Prince Interrupted. "We've Known Each Other For A Long, Long Time. It's Imperative That Your Associates Understand How Critical It Is. Please Understand, You Are A Good Friend. But, I Am Deeply Saddened To Say This Project Is Beyond Our Friendship." Urgency Was Apparent In The Prince's Statement, And Firmness Was In His Hand As He Reached Out To Seward's And Patted It. "We Cannot Allow Our Friendship To Stand In The Way Of, Shall We Say, Our Two Countries' Accomplishments?"

Seward Covered The Prince's Hand With His Own. "Acknowledged, Old Buddy." He Stood And Stretched A Kink From His Muscular Shoulder. "I'll Call You Tomorrow. With Good News."

"To Your Health, My Good Friend."

As Seward Turned, The Prince Raised His Glass And Brought It Back To The Table Without Taking A Sip, Keeping Eye Contact With Seward While Nodding Toward Two Ladies In A Nearby Table. "Make It Later In The Day, Daniel. I May Take Them Racing."

* * * * * * * *

The tires screeched as the white Corvette accelerated out of the pits. Bits of spray, left from the overnight dew, flew from the wide tires as they squealed toward the first curve It was just a practice day, but it was always race time for Prince Anini. To stay in good racing form, he needed a competitor, a fierce one. And, if none were available, his imagination would pit him against Michael Andretti.

He was closing the gap and had to make his move before turn two or it was all over for this race. His foot in the throttle, he approached curve one and hit second as he turned on more power. The Corvette's soft racing slicks gripped the asphalt. He brought the powerful machine's nose around the curve and headed for the straight. Third gear propelled him even faster as he shoved the pedal to the floorboards. He was gaining. His pulse raced as the car screamed down the straightaway. He was going for top end. He hit fourth and the tires squeaked as they responded to the five hundred horses under the fiberglass hood. He let up on the gas to balance the car's weight as he downshifted to third, in preparation for the ninety-degree turn. He quickly glanced to the tachometer, and realized his rpm were too high for his position on the track. It was far too fast. He hit the brakes, but he felt no response. The brake pedal crashed to the floorboard with a crunching sound as the prince's worst fears were about to be realized. At 120 mph, he crashed head on into the concrete barrier. The Corvette erupted into a ball of flame as it disintegrated, taking the prince and the shy young woman with it. Last night she had no idea what today's cruel fate had in store for her.

Frantically, the pit crew rushed to the crash scene. One crew member remained in the pits—a small, dark man with black curly hair and suspicious eyes. The aroma of brake fluid still on his hands, Jopaq wiped his forehead with a shop rag, tossed it into a barrel, and simply walked away.

* * * * * * * * * *

Across the Potomac in downtown Washington, the D.C. field office of Turner Engineering Corporation occupied the top floor of a five-story building on "I" Street, just north of Massachusetts Avenue. Erected on a set of massive concrete columns, the street level was for parking only, cars entering from all four sides. The only car remaining in the lot was a light blue Mercedes sedan. The license plate read "TURNER." Daniel Seward parked in the stall next to the Mercedes. The elevator door opened directly into the Turner reception area. Seward stepped onto the thick gray carpet. It smelled new.

Two room dividers separated the reception area; a desk was centered between them. In front of each divider was a pair of Hawaiian palms growing from matching clay pots. Except for a phone, the reception desk was clean. A custodian's cart stood in the middle of the room, empty baskets next to the cart. The power cord from the Hoover stretched across the room to a socket next to the elevator door. Several black plastic bags lay bulging next to the cart waiting to be carried to the basement dumpster.

The open area beyond the reception desk contained rows of cluttered desks. Beyond them, a row of beige file cabinets filled the wall next to a hallway that led off to the right. At the end of the hallway was the office of the company president, Kenneth Turner. Seward stood outside the door. He peered in, anxious.

Turner sat at his desk. His chin was resting in both palms. A brilliant engineer from Princeton, he'd earned an advanced degree in nuclear physics. But tonight he wasn't sure if he knew the difference between a nuclear sub and a rowboat.

At barely five feet five and 135 pounds, the 47-year-old, alcoholic-turned teetotaler surprised everyone. Those who had first watched him on the five o'clock news and later met him in person were surprised at his size. In part, what made him look taller was his face. A square jaw, thick brows and heavy mustache, he had a full head of silver hair, and his posture demonstrated that his ego was, indeed, self-important. Naturally, his hair was in place and perfectly combed. He had mastered the use of heavy sunglasses as a prop that, he thought, made him even more authoritative. He was an absolute genius in the field of nuclear weaponry, and, as such, he was also the world's expert in the design of tracking systems to detect one of his incoming weapons, should the need arise. One of the tracking systems is now resting on the Atlantic Ocean floor.

Startled, he looked up as Seward entered the office. "Daniel."

"Sorry to bother you, Ken." Seward walked inside the office to the desk. "You look like a whipped puppy. Got a minute?"

Turner leaned back to a near-reclining posture. The elegant leather chair squeaked. "Can I get you something? Scotch?"

"Nothing, thank you." Seward walked to the window and looked out at the city lights.

The outline of the Government Printing Office against the twinkling city lights was a fitting backdrop to the deal-making these two were involved in. He turned to face Turner. "We have a problem."

"I sympathize with you—"

"Sympathize?" Seward interrupted. "Like the man said, you'll find that in the dictionary somewhere around shit and suicide! I don't want your sympathy. I want the system."

"I realize that. But we've got a situation here…"

"Bet your sweet rear end. It was FOB Frankfurt, Ken. Sad thing is, it never made it. The way I see it, it's your problem. You and Bortens screwed up big time—"

"Now wait a minute," Turner interrupted. "I've been on the damn phone all day with Bortens. They're as baffled as I am."

"Come on Ken. For God's sake man."

"There's something strange going down. Take the FAA, for instance."

"Why's that?"

"They're quiet as hell. They're not talking. To anybody. It's like somebody got to them."

"How?"

"I have an idea or two. But, I'm afraid that Bortens doesn't know what to think. Frankly, I'm not sure I do either."

In the corner, next to a straight back chair, stood an antique table. Its dark oak legs curved gracefully to the carpet. In the middle of the glass top and in contrast to its design, was an elegant chrome lamp. Seward sat in the hard chair next to the table and switched on the lamp. A warm light filled the room.

"Damn it, Ken, we have a good deal that's gone bad. It was supposed to have been delivered in thirty days, installed and working."

"I know," replied Turner. "And I also know it would take us twice that time to build another one."

"We can't wait," argued Seward. "Besides, I'm really concerned about the one sitting on the bottom of the ocean."

"I know," Turner replied. "Bortens's recovery team is supposedly on their way now. Besides, I have another concern."

"Same as mine?" Seward asked.

"You guessed it," said Turner. "It can't fall into anyone else's hands."

"It's not just our concern. How about the entire country?" Seward paused. "How could Bortens be so damned careless?"

"Dan, I can't believe it," Turner said. "With their record? They've flown missions for everyone. You name them. Our government, their government, everybody's government, and just about anybody who's anybody."

Seward shook his head. "Must be the CIA."

"Look. President Fenimore is a bright enough man, but I question his judgment sometimes." Turner paused to interpret Seward's questioned look. "Really, Dan, think about it. He appointed Cavalli to head up the CIA, and he wasn't even qualified for the job."

"True enough, Cavalli's a loser," Seward replied. "You suppose he caught the president having sex with a pig?"

"No other way," agreed Turner.

"Take a look at him. He's a savvy enough guy when it comes to foreign policy and domestic issues, but admittedly Fenimore, or any other president for that matter, doesn't know his butt from home plate when it comes to the intelligence community. He's not even plugged into the community." He sighed. "Hell, maybe Cavalli's OK, I don't know. But bottom line, Fenimore has no control over him. In fact, no president has ever controlled the CIA. They're not even members of the Intelligenc Board. Case in point? Remember Nixon and Watergate? A couple of those were tagged as Company guys, but you know as well as I, that they were retired. That would be the only way Nixon could've pulled it off."

"I believe it," Turner agreed.

"Even besides all that, he's beind in the polls, so what good does any of this do for him?" Seward caught his breath.

"Another term!" Turner said.

"Sure," Seward agreed. "He actually thinks he's doing the country a service by spearheading this whole Saudi thing. Think about it. Cavalli must be in agreement?"

"Well then, Ken. They're all in this together. Must be. Fenimore's in favor of the deal and, who knows, maybe the whole community is too."

"I'm not sure." Turner stood and walked to the window. "But I suppose you're right."

"Sure. Look at it this way," added Seward. "First of all, I doubt if he would strike out on his own and do something without his advisors' consent. True, the First Lady picks out his skivvies, but he's not that stupid, except on intelligence matters."

"I gather Fenimore's not getting your vote?" Turner quipped, shaking his head. He massaged the bridge of his nose with a thumb and little finger. "I don't know about that relationship."

"So what's the other alternative?" asked Seward. "When you think real hard about it, the CIA couldn't have been involved because, no matter what, everyone has the same motivation. Don't you think Bortens just screwed up?"

"That's my guess," replied Turner. "But I'll have to withhold my judgment until tomorrow."

"In any event, no matter who or why, we made a promise," said Seward. "Well, let's say the president made a promise. The Saudis want the goods. And, it's in both of our best interests to provide them. After all, it's big bucks for us, you know."

"I'll have to agree on that one Dan," said Turner. You should know more than anyone, after being the Pentagon's eyes and ears in the Middle East for a long time."

"I agree with the president on one thing at least," Seward stated. "The Saudis are our one key element in bringing peace to the region. Besides, Fenimore asked for my help, and my client needs another system. Fast."

"I'll speak to the president," Turner promised.

Seward stood and buttoned the middle button of his brown suit jacket and straightened his tie. Over the years, he had learned not to irritate the smaller, more emotional president of Turner Engineering. "You're right, you know. It's politics, old boy. Pure, unadulterated, down-home, freaking' politics. As we speak, our tax dollars are no doubt being well spent on the prince's behalf and maybe the wife of some ambassador."

"At least we both agree on one thing," said Turner.

"That's for damn sure. By the way—"

The phone rang. Turner held up an index finger. "Let me get this." He raised the phone. "Yes. What? When? Did they say how? Oh, for God's sake!" He stopped talking and after a short pause, he continued. "I suppose we can. I'll tell him."

He replaced the receiver and stared out the window. The room grew cold. He turned to Seward and shook his head. "Anini is dead."

Seward looked at Turner in disbelief. "What?"

"A car crash. At the track."

Seward's mind raced as anxiety overcame him. He paced the thick carpet, and suddenly he froze. He massaged his jaw with his index finger and thumb while thoughts raced through his mind. What about the system? Was the king behind the deal? And what about the king? "Do they know how?"

"He hit the wall," explained Turner. "He was doing over a hundred. It exploded into a ball of fire. That's all they said."

"Oh my God, Ken. We must meet with the king. Right away."

"We? That's your game, Daniel. But if you need any help, I'll do what I can."

Seward turned to leave but stopped. "I'll be in touch. But just in case, you'd better get busy."

A few minutes later, Seward turned his Lincoln west on Massachusetts and went deep into thought, reflecting on his tennis partner. They had known each other personally and professionally for years and had shared offices in Frankfurt. He was in a bind and needed to confirm his next move with the king.

* * * * * * * * * *

Amacon Electric was the only tenant in the one level office building. Kirby Road ran east and west at a point about three miles south of Langley. The office was low profile— no fancy sidewalk, no fancy signs. Just an older brick building. A gravel shoulder separated the asphalt from the curb. A faint amber glow could be seen from one of the windows. The other was dark. Two cars were parked in the small gravel lot. One was a new Seville and the other a Lincoln limo. A man in a dark suit leaned against the limo's front fender. He lit a cigarette and shook the match until its fire went out, then flicked it to the gravel. He kept a watchful eye on the road.

Inside the unpretentious office building, two men were in a heated discussion; one was Allen Adams, president of Amacon Electric. An intense man in his late forties, the tall, rugged man was a fast mover. He got things done and hated being around anyone who couldn't measure up to his own performance standards.

The receiver of Adams's wrath was Dieter Albrecht, attorney-at-law. An immigrant from Berlin, his father had been convicted of treason against Hitler and had lived the remainder of his life in a concentration camp. Years later, after living from day to day in poverty, his mother led him and his sister through a tunnel under the Berlin Wall where they eventually found their freedom. His relentless networking helped him land a scholarship at Harvard Law School where he was a whiz kid, recognized for his intelligence and craftiness at manipulating the law to suit his needs. He was short with straight blond hair.

"Look, damn it, you'd better wrap this thing up now. We've taken care of one, but don't let that fool you into some sort of half-assed complacency." Adams was furious. "Do you understand, Mein Herr?"

Albrecht held his breath. He wanted to tell Adams to kiss off, but in spite of his short fuse, he held his temper. "I'm working on it." He hated Adams, especially for mocking his German ancestry.

"Is that all you can say? That's an admission of nothing. We need the girl at once. Now! Today, without delay! Can I make myself any more clear?"

Albrecht was ready to strike but recoiled again. It took every ounce of control to restrain himself. He wanted so much to shoot Adams between the eyes, but he remained calm and took the harassment. If he failed, a cold slab of concrete in a remote Hinterland prison camp would be far less harsh than anything his American employers would dispense. No way would he fail in this or any other Amacon assignment.

FIVE

Lower Manhattan—the southern tip of New York City, from Rockefeller Center to the Battery—was a four-mile stage of deadly undercurrents and real bad guys. In the old days of sailing ships, many an unsuspecting sailor, drunk on rum, would awake to the surprising smell of salty air, a victim of a midnight shanghai, dragged from his bed in the gutter down a dark and slimy alley, through one of several secret tunnels to a three-masted bark anchored off the lowest point on the island. Why? Profits. The only difference between then and now was that, now, the key players wore three-piece suits. However, today's situation was much the same. It was the birthplace of the white collar version of organized crime. On a daily basis, trade secrets and bullets were exchanged in boardrooms that numbered as many as there are bad guys.

Broadway ran north from the Customs House, splitting the island in two. Some said if the happening was going to happen, it would do so on Broadway. A few blocks off Broadway, though, the city's nerve center pulsated with every murder, burglary, and rape. Broadway was its spinal cord that carried its grim messages deep into the concrete jungle.

Off the street and behind the boardroom doors, the pulsations were unique. Here, it was a closed show on a need-to-know basis, and the public wasn't invited. Their cash might well have been at stake, but they never had a vote. Stock manipulation was either a direct or indirect result of a trade secret gone to a competitor. Big dollars were at play in this arena. And, there was no public outcry from the victims of corporate espionage. Never.

Even the best-guarded secret sold on the street was done so without a leak to the press. Every time a corporation was screwed out of something dear, it was done so by an unbelievably talented cast of characters who had their reasons for doing the screwing. And it all boiled down to the same thing, big bucks. What was more, being discovered wasn't in their game plan. Even more deadly than the street gangs, they silenced anyone, anytime, to cover their tracks. And they were as good at it as their government counterparts who had once roamed the Communist-bordered countries of Europe and Asia. If you were a player, your stage was a dangerous place. If you were a clerk-typist, their deadly games were being played all around you, without your even suspecting.

Lower Manhattan was, indeed, a place to behold. From here, major decisions were made that affect the lives of people throughout the city and, yes, throughout the country.

City Hall, the state office buildings, the Federal Reserve, Wall Street. They were all here, including the courthouse. The steps leading there were crowded with attorneys and their clients bustling to one of the many courtrooms inside. Bill Gale and Sam Rader had finished a quick lunch and were now a part of that crowd.

Judge Thomas Rickey's chambers were situated on the third floor. The courtroom was relatively quiet. A young Latino couple was seated in the back row in the middle, a teenage mother occupied the back row next to the aisle, and a pair of elderly couples sat at the far end of the middle row. A young woman entered through the doors and slid across the front-row pew, the rubber soles of her sneakers squeaking on the white marble floor.

Recessed fluorescent fixtures provided additional light for the otherwise sunny courtroom. Leaded glass windows reached to the ceiling. The other three walls were embossed with a gray, flowery print over a sea of gray. The wallpaper was as old as the mahogany wainscoting. A spindle barricade ran the width of the courtroom, except for a gate in the middle.

Gale followed Rader through the gate to the table on the left. He sat in one of the three oak chairs and folded his hands on the table's varnished surface. He wondered what was next. Rader took a manila file folder from his briefcase and laid it on the table. He closed his case and placed it on the tile floor and remained standing.

Dieter Albrecht walked into the courtroom like a man with a purpose. His steady eyes looked straight ahead as he walked through the gate and took his place at the plaintiff's table. He had a single leather folder from which he removed a file folder and placed both on the desk, file folder on top. He never acknowledged his opponents. He slowly walked to one of the tall windows, gazed to the street for a minute, then returned to his table and stood there leaning against it. Right down to his polished wingtips, he looked the part of a hot-shot lawyer—couldn't lose, quick decisions, always right…click, click, click, done. He gave a quick glance to Rader and methodically returned his eyes to the file before him.

Responding to Gale's nudge, Rader raised an eyebrow and whispered, "Albrecht. Dieter Albrecht."

"Does he know we're here?" Gale asked, jokingly.

"He knows all right. You watch him. He's no pushover, I'm told. This could be an interesting couple of days."

"Is she here?" asked Gale.

Rader twisted his shoulders to look around the courtroom until he spotted Dominique Fabours come through the doors. He stood and walked to her, meeting her in the aisle. He took her hand and led her to the first pew behind the barricade. Her hands were trembling. Reassuringly, he slightly tightened his grip and whispered, "Just relax now. I doubt if you'll take the stand this afternoon. Probably in the morning. Sit tight." As she took her seat, Rader returned to the defendant's table.

"That's Dominique," said Rader.

"Great." Gale turned to get a better look at Bortens's chief of operations and liked what he saw. She was dark with shiny black hair pulled back from her face. Under forty, he thought, but not by much. Her high cheekbones accentuated her narrow, dark eyes. He placed her in some remote South Pacific island. Maybe Tahiti.

As Judge Rickey entered the room, the bailiff cried out, "All rise. The court of Judge Thomas Rickey please come to order. All those having business in this courtroom state that ye shall speak and seek the truth." The judge took his seat behind a large and very old oak desk. The bailiff continued, "Please be seated."

As those in the room took their seats, Gale watched the judge shuffle the papers on his desk, seeming to arrange them in some fashion or another. Gale made a few mental notes. The judge seemed to be a fair enough looking man—hopefully fair enough to rule in favor of his client. The judge appeared to be over six feet tall, a slight paunch, and maybe in his late sixties. No beard or mustache, round jawed, thin lips, and fair skin. Not much sun. Probably read a lot. Gale leaned back, ready for the action.

Judge Rickey held a paper at arm's length and studied it for a moment. He glanced at both the plaintiff and defendant tables, raised his eyebrows, and let out a breath. He addressed the two attorneys. "Gentlemen. Are we ready to proceed?"

Albrecht stood and addressed the bench, "Plaintiff is ready, Your Honor."

Rader echoed his adversary, "Your Honor, we're ready as well."

The judge studied the paper in his hands. "Gentlemen, as I read here, this court is to decide the amount of settlement Bortens is to pay. And this settlement shall be based on the facts of the case including negligence, if any, on the part of the defendant. I have in front of me the findings of the Federal Aviation Administration. I assume you both have copies?" The judge looked up from the paper at the two attorneys.

"Plaintiff has copies, Your Honor."

"Likewise, Your Honor," Rader replied.

Judge Rickey continued. "Good. Then let's get down to business. I see we have a half hour set aside for today with more time this week. Will that be sufficient gentlemen?"

"That will be fine," Rader replied.

Albrecht studied the papers in front of him.

"Mr. Albrecht. Is this sufficient for you?" The judge prompted.

"Excuse me, Your Honor. Yes, that is sufficient for now."

"For now? When we leave this courtroom, I assume we'll all be in accord, Mr. Albrecht."

"Oh, yes sir. Excuse me," Albrecht stumbled. "I meant that is sufficient for the plaintiff, Your Honor."

"I see there is only one witness registered for this case," said the judge. "Is this correct, gentlemen?"

"That is correct," replied Rader.

"Plaintiff has no witnesses registered with the court, Your Honor. The FAA report will serve as ours."

Gale elbowed Rader, who responded with a shrug. "I don't know, Bill. If that's all he's got, we shouldn't have much trouble tomorrow."

"Because of the time and the court's schedule, today I'll hear the plaintiff's case, and tomorrow you may present yours. Gentlemen, if we have only one witness to present, do either of you feel we need to schedule time past tomor-row?"

Rader responded first. "Your Honor, our presentation should take only about half of a day at most. Unless cross-examination is longer than that, defendant can see no rea-son to tie up the court's time beyond tomorrow."

"And you, Mr. Albrecht?" the judge inquired.

"No sir, I believe tomorrow will be sufficient," replied Albrecht.

"Well, gentlemen, let's proceed. Mr. Albrecht, it's your courtroom."

Albrecht stood, pushed the chair back, and slowly walked around the table and leaned against the front of it. He planted both feet firmly on the floor. His slacks were neatly creased. He seemed youthful and yet had the look of one who had been on the streets for a while. He ran his fin-gers through a head of straight blond hair and studied the floor.

He directed his attention to the judge. "Your Honor, plaintiff is asking the court to award five hundred thousand dollars for each of the families of the two deceased pilots, per their contract." He paused and cleared his throat, then continued. "And nine million dollars punitive damages as a result of negligence by Bortens Air Cargo. To be split equally between the two families."

Albrecht glanced toward the window, then to the judge. He continued, "Plaintiff will prove that Bortens was negli-gent in the loading of the aircraft to the extent that it caused the aircraft to shift in flight which, then, was the cause of the crash. If you read the report, you would see what I mean, Your Honor."

"Mr. Albrecht, I certainly hope the court's capability to both read and comprehend this particular report is not the point of this presentation. In any event, you may continue."

"Excuse me, Your Honor. I didn't mean to infer…"

"Please continue, Mr. Albrecht. By the way, do you have any evidence to prove the allegation that Bortens was negligent? That is, other than the FAA report?"

"No, Your Honor," Albrecht replied. "The report is the basis for our case against Bortens—"

"Your Honor," Rader stood up. "We move to dismiss."

"Not quite so fast, Mr. Rader. As with any document so prepared by government employees, the report could be construed in any number of ways. It's poorly written at best. So, for our education, at least, I'll allow Mr. Albrecht to continue. Mr. Albrecht, please."

Gale caught a glimpse of Albrecht's smile, which he suspected wasn't meant to be seen by anyone. Perhaps he knew something about the FAA's report that neither the judge nor Rader had spotted. The question was, what was it, and why didn't he mention it now? It appeared to him there wasn't much of a case except for the FAA report. He knew that part of Rader's defense was the testimony of Dominique.

By now, Albrecht's moves were becoming more predictable to Gale. Again he walked to the side of the table, and again he looked toward the windows and back to the manila folders on the table. "Your Honor, in his report, Mr. Wilson states the cause of the crash to be pilot error. And, in addition, the summary of such evidence would lead a reasonable man to conclude the simple fact that the pilots, while perhaps not having much of a chance, had added to their fate, a load that shifted so suddenly and with such force that the aircraft simply couldn't right itself, no matter the skills of the pilots, God rest their souls. So, it appears we have both negligent loading and pilot error." Another stare at the window and he was back to the table, occupying the same space. "Now, we realize that the plane is down deep enough to make recovery impossible. Without physical evidence to the contrary, plaintiffs request that the court decide in favor of plaintiffs." Albrecht sat down. He was finished.

Judge Rickey gave Albrecht a puzzled look. "Mr. Albrecht, is the court to assume this is the sum of your case?"

Albrecht stood and faced the judge. "Yes sir. Mr. Wilson's summary agrees with…"

"Mr. Albrecht, Mr. Wilson's narrative is nothing more than a personal opinion of an event to which he has no more first-hand knowledge than you or I. It's a summary of the so-called facts as he has interpreted them. It's not proof in any way, shape, or form. And, Mr. Albrecht, this judge reads far more into the report than apparently you do. I am tempted to grant the families their normal settlement by Bortens which, I might add, is generous." He turned a page and continued. "More than the liability limits, per the contract. And furthermore, I am tempted to dismiss the punitive damages for lack of, let's say, presentation by you, Mr. Albrecht. But rather than doing so at this juncture, I'll allow you until tomorrow morning to put together a case. Because right now, yours is lacking. Do I make myself clear?"

Albrecht had sat down for his scolding, and, after inserting the papers into their files and then into a leather folder, he stood to face the judge. "I understand, sir. I apologize for taking the court's time in what may appear, at first, to be a frivolous suit for punitive damages. Tomorrow I shall present additional facts to prove that Mr. Wilson's summaries are more than mere opinions."

"Fine then. Gentlemen, if there are no further items to discuss, I'll see you first thing in the morning." He rapped his gavel.

As Rader collected the papers into his briefcase, Gale glanced at Albrecht who glanced back, smiling. No question about it, Albrecht was up to something. But what?

"Let's grab a cab and get out of here," Rader said, heading out the door with Gale and Dominique close behind. Once outside the courtroom, he introduced them. "Oh by the way, may I present Dominique. Dominique, Gale." A cab screeched to a stop in front of them, and they climbed into the back seat. Rader gave instructions to the driver, and the cab headed uptown toward the Regency Hotel.

A few car lengths behind, another cab followed. Its only paying occupant was a small, precise man with black, curly hair and piercing oriental eyes. The pursuing cab followed a few car lengths behind, switching lanes to shield itself from being spotted.

Jopaq reached inside his coat pocket and retrieved a small-bore automatic. The silencer was in place. He would wait for the right moment. Onto Franklin Roosevelt Drive and north along the East River at a moderate speed, both cabs took the exit at the Queensboro Bridge and headed west on 60th toward Central Park. Jopaq opened the right side window, his automatic hidden under a newspaper, safety off. He waited for an opportunity.

The first cab pulled to the curb and stopped in front of the Regency Hotel. Gale was the first out of the cab and onto the sidewalk, where he turned to check traffic and saw the other cab that was dangerously close. Instinctively, he shouted at Rader and Dominique, pointing to the curb. "This side! Get out this side!"

But Rader had already opened his side. Without hesitating, he closed it moments before the other cab came within inches of the precise spot where Rader would have been standing.

"That was a close one." Rader thanked him. Neither were aware that the close call was no accident.

Maybe next time, Jopaq thought to himself. There will be plenty more opportunities.

At that time of day, about three in the afternoon, the bar was quiet. A man and woman, both dressed in business attire, were in one of the corner booths. Their eyes were so busy staring into each other's that they were unaware of anyone else. The bartender was talking software to the only other patron, a young man in a business suit and dark horn-rimmed glasses. At the end of the bar, a TV set hung precariously from the ceiling by two chains. It was tuned to the afternoon news. It provided most of the light for the darkened room, but the volume was so low, it could barely be heard above the bartender's southern drawl. Gale caught only part of it.

"The President's popularity...gaining in foreign policy...White House reports today that agreements have been reached...Saudi government helps promote peace in the Middle East...top-secret guidance system...10,000 new jobs provided by Turner Engineering ..."

They took one of the middle tables. Rader signaled the waiter as Gale held the chair for Dominique. He noticed her gracefulness as she walked, and even more now that she sat down. Gale became quickly aware of her youthful figure. "So tell me, Dominique, are you a native of New York?"

She straightened her skirt and placed her elbows on the table. "I've lived here for the past five years. Originally, I'm from New Orleans, was transferred to San Francisco. But now I live here."

"Oh, then you worked in Bortens head office?" Gale asked, already knowing the answer.

"I've been with Bortens for about twelve years." Dominique's skin was tanned and smooth.

"You said New Orleans?" Gale asked.

"Yes. I was born there. My father had emigrated from France before the war, and my mother was a mixture of Cajun and French Indian."

"I see." Gale continued to stare.

"Maybe Sam told you." She looked at Rader who nodded. "I'm the operations manager for Bortens. I see that our aircraft are on time and have full cargoes, are loaded properly, things like that."

Five

"Like?"

"I'm afraid so."

Rader led the conversation. "Why don't we go over tomorrow's agenda? I don't know what our counterpart is up to, and to be perfectly honest with you, I'm bothered about him."

"I think I see what you mean," Gale agreed. "He's a shifty one."

"That he is," Rader said as he massaged the bridge of his nose with thumb and forefinger. "But, there's not much we can do except tell our story." He addressed Dominique. "I just want you to describe the loading procedure and how you followed it by the book. I believe you wrote the book." Both elbows resting on the table, Rader clasped his hands in front of his face and nibbled on both thumbs. "Why don't you tell Bill about it?"

She took in a deep breath and let it out. "The plane was loaded properly. It's not such a big deal anyway. The whole procedure is pretty much automatic. It's common sense to our crew."

"Is it possible to load it any other way?" Gale questioned.

"There aren't any. But didn't they hint at pilot error as the probable cause?" she asked Rader.

"That's what the FAA says in its report, if you can believe it. There's simply no way. Pilot error on takeoff? If there was ever an adrenaline rush, that would be the time and, of course, that would be the time our pilots are the most alert. Then, once they're at altitude, the aircraft pretty much flies itself."

"What about the shift in cargo?" she asked, then answered her own question. "Of course, procedurally, everything was done correctly. The cargo just couldn't have shifted. No, I simply can't imagine that happening."

"Tell me about a cargo shift." Gale shrugged his massive shoulders. "How could that happen?"

Dominique spoke with authority. She knew her subject well. "Generally speaking, under normal conditions, even if the cargo weren't tied down, any shift could hardly be serious enough to cause what happened in this case. Besides, I know how it was loaded. I was there—"

"I'm sorry, but I don't understand," Gale interrupted. "You're losing me. Why would you be there? I mean, on this particular flight? Do you physically inspect every cargo that flies out of there?"

"No. And that's a very good point. The manifest asked for a physical inspection at the time of loading."

"Isn't that unusual?" Gale asked.

"Not necessarily, Mr. Gale. We handle cargo for some very special and rather unique customers."

"Like for instance?"

Rather than answer right away, Dominique looked to Rader for his blessing. Getting it, she continued. "Like the government. Much of our cargo goes to areas that are either bounded by or supported by the Soviets."

"Korea?" asked Gale.

"China, Russia, Middle East," she added.

Dominique seemed to show no restraint in talking about the delivery points that, at this point, meant nothing to him. It was the cargo that piqued his interest. What was it? Who was it for? And what did it cost? If he was going to help, he needed the answers. For now, though, he figured it best to wait for a more opportune time to ask for more. After all, he'd like to get to know her better, and what would it hurt any to mix business with pleasure? If he played his cards right, his questions would be answered at the right time.

"Tell me about the loading," Gale asked. "Was it centered properly? How was it secured?"

"Everything was fine. The cargo was secured properly. Everything was perfect. I knew the captain very well. We were joking about something or another as the cargo was being loaded. As much as I try, I just can't explain why it went down. This is a first for me." She sniffed gently, glanced at Rader, then smiled at Gale. "I'm so sorry. This is all pretty devastating."

Rader put his hand on hers. "Now don't you worry about a thing. You'll do fine tomorrow."

Gale had been studying her throughout their conversation, and, although he couldn't put his finger on it, something wasn't right. Her emotions seemed genuine, but he wondered if she was concerned about the blame being focused on her; or could it be the loss of the crew or the plane?

Gale moved on. "So, Sam, what about tomorrow?"

Rader returned his glass to the wet napkin where it had been resting. "Tomorrow is sure to be an interesting day. Apparently, Albrecht's only play is the FAA's contention that the cause was pilot error. But our presentation, mainly Dominique's, should set the record straight about the loading, and I don't want to forget the abilities of the pilots as well."

"I see."

"We'll contend that the aircraft was loaded properly and present the crew's credentials, while Albrecht gives the FAA report."

"So it's basically up to the judge?" asked Gale.

"You've got it. Whoever presents the most believable case wins! Pure and simple, we've got to convince old Rickey that we're also honest and way aboveboard."

"Thrifty, brave, clean, and reverent."

"You've got it again." Rader turned to Dominique. "So tomorrow, I want you to tell exactly what you saw and did at the terminal. And all you know about the pilots. Nothing more, nothing less. That's it. But I must warn you to be careful of Albrecht. I haven't the slightest idea of what he's up to. He'll try to pull something. Maybe in his cross-examination; I don't know for sure. But let's not worry about that now. Just be yourself, and Rickey will love you." Rader stood to stretch out the kinks then pulled a gold pen from his shirt pocket. "Well gang, let's do it. Want us to drop you somewhere, Dominique?"

"No. I'll get a cab. It's not far to my home."

As Rader paid the check, Gale escorted her from the bar. On their way, something in one of the booths caught Gale's attention. Except for the couple in the corner and one man at the bar, the place was empty when they entered and, to his recollection, no one entered or left the bar since they sat down. He would have known. He had sat at the table with his back against the wall. Also, every booth had a lit candle on the table. They were all the same, red with white netting around its base. But the one on that particular table had been blown out.

A small man sat alone, facing away, drinking from a cup. Gale studied him for a second and thought it was strange how he kept the cup to his lips for such a long time. It was dark and his face was hidden, but not his curly hair. Gale dismissed it for the time being and shifted his attention to Dominique.

Once in the lobby, they waited for Rader, who joined them at the revolving door. As Rader again reassured her about tomorrow's day in court, he must have thought she was in good hands because he said his good nights and headed through the lobby and into a waiting elevator. She took Gale's arm, and he escorted her outside. By then it was dark. As much as he was enamored with his new acquaintance, he found he couldn't dismiss the man in the bar. His appearance was a bit too much out of context.

Gale told Dominique to wait as he checked it out. He rushed back into the bar to find it empty, but the candle now burning. He rushed to the men's room, carefully slipped the door partially open. No one there. He returned to the bar, where he surveyed every booth, but he found no trace of the man. Funny, Gale thought, there was no place to hide and no place to go. Only one way in and one way out.

Unsatisfied but suspicious, Gale returned to Dominique, who was standing at the curb as a cab drove up. He opened the door for her, said goodbye, and watched the cab as it headed toward Greenwich Village. He bought a *New York Times* from the curbside vendor and scanned the front page.

> *President Fenimore's popularity gaining in foreign policy. America shares latest military strategies with Saudi allies…jobs created by Turner Engineering…*

He stood for a moment, continuing to read the top half of the folded paper. He flipped it over and scanned the bottom half, completely oblivious of the other man, watching from a half block away.

The cab pulled to a stop in front of a mid-century apartment building in the heart of the Village, where Dominique got out, paid the cabby, and looked down the street. Several jazz bars were in full swing. A few people were gathered under a brightly-lit facade that announced tonight's blues concert. Without checking her watch, she knew it was a little past seven. By eight, the line would be much longer, and by eight-thirty, the place would be jumping. A neighbor's cat purred innocently as it rubbed its head against the wrought iron railing leading up to the double entry doors of her apartment building.

She was startled by a lone figure on the landing at the top of the stairs but somewhat relieved that he wore a business suit. She tightened her grip on her purse. She was accustomed to living in Manhattan. She kept her eyes pointed at the man as she reached the landing.

He shifted his weight and cleared his throat. "I'm sorry to startle you, Miss Fabours. Very sorry." He stepped away from the wall where the street light made him visible. "I'm Dieter Albrecht. Can we speak for a moment?"

"What are you doing here?" Dominique asked. "You're not supposed to—"

"I know," Albrecht pleaded as he reached out and touched her hand.

Defiantly, she moved back out of touch. She was puzzled. "I'm not certain I understand why you are here. It's late and—"

He withdrew his arm. "Please don't be alarmed. I realize I'm breaking the most sacred rules of legal protocol. But I think I have something that may interest you."

At this moment, she wasn't sure what to do, so she made a choice to hear him out. She'd watched him in court, and no matter how smoothly he talked, she wouldn't be fooled. He was very cagey. She sensed evil in the way he moved and the way he spoke. She remembered Rader's warning as she said, "Please be brief. It's late, and I have plenty to do."

"I think we can help each other. You see, I have a problem, and I truly believe that your help in solving it would bring us both some very good benefits. Shall I continue?"

"I suppose so."

"The point is this," Albrecht said. "My client is asking for you to alter your testimony. Just a little."

She grabbed the rail. "What are you saying?"

"Please relax, Miss Fabours. I don't mean to offend you, but please hear me out."

"Mr. Albrecht, we're not supposed to be talking. You know very well—"

"I realize that, and I am deeply apologetic for contacting you in this manner," Albrecht reiterated. "But please let me explain. Will you hear me out?"

By this time, Albrecht's smile had warmed her to the extent that she may as well hear what he had to say. She was sure of herself and where she stood in the matter but decided to listen. Then she'd ask him to leave. "All right then. Make it fast; then be on your way."

"Thank you for listening," Albrecht said. "I'm sure you won't be sorry. It's all pretty simple, but here's what we're offering you. We'd like you to state that while loading, you noticed two defective tie-downs and raised this point to your bosses, only to be shot down."

Dominique looked down and shook her head. "You are asking me to lie? Why on earth would I ever…?"

"Now please, Miss Fabours. Please bear with me for just a few more seconds." Albrecht looked both ways, then lowered his voice. "You see, there really were two defective tie-downs, and they did break, causing the load to shift and the plane to crash. You, being the honest and forthright employee that you are, called San Francisco and told your bosses that the plane would have to be off-loaded and the defective equipment replaced. In all, it would have caused a two-day delay because the parts, the tie-downs, were on back order somewhere. But they told you to approve the shipment anyway, and that they'd accept all responsibility. Now if you want, Miss Fabours, you don't even have to say you talked to your boss. Make something up. Like you talked to a purchasing agent. Make it believable."

She fidgeted with the top button of her blouse as she tried to calm down. "I can't believe you're saying this. First of all, it never happened. This equipment simply doesn't break. I can't think of anytime—"

"Miss Fabours, please stop," urged Albrecht. "And don't miss the point. We don't presume to understand your business in the slightest. Plus that, I doubt if the judge understands it any better than we do. And to add to the difficulties, I doubt if Mr. Rader understands any of the technical stuff either. The point is simply this. We need your help."

Dominique relaxed momentarily and responded, "For sake of argument. Let's say I go along with it. Then what?"

"Ah. I knew you'd be interested."

"I didn't say I was interested," Dominique replied. "I'm just listening."

"I see. So, here's the good part. My clients will give you five hundred thousand dollars."

She gasped, and her mouth dropped before she caught herself. "Excuse me. I didn't mean—"

"It's quite all right, Miss Fabours," Albrecht continued. "A half-million dollars. I assume you have a place for it?"

"Who wouldn't? That's a lot of money." Dominique caught her breath. "An awful lot."

Albrecht reached out to shake her hand in agreement. "Do we have a deal then?" His hand remained extended for a moment, alone. "Can we count on you tomorrow?"

The crowd was building as the cabs unloaded their fares in midstreet. The pandemonium from hundreds of happy ticket holders filled the evening air, pierced occasionally by a wailing siren and a honk from an irate motorist. Dominique was up all night trying to come up with her decision.

SIX

Judge Rickey arranged the papers on his desk in preparation for the hearing. "Are we ready to proceed, gentlemen?"

"Ready, Your Honor," Albrecht replied as he glanced first to the defendant's table, then to Dominique, who was seated in the first row, directly behind the Bortens defense table.

Gale caught Albrecht's glance and followed it to Dominique, where her eyes met his, then drifted to the far side of the courtroom. Gale noticed that those wonderfully tanned cheeks of hers suddenly turned crimson. Maybe he'd made an impression? Whatever it was would have to wait.

"Defendant is ready, Your Honor," Rader replied.

Judge Rickey recapped the events of the day before, which weren't all that impressive since, in Gale's mind, nothing much had happened. But he continued scrutinizing Albrecht, balancing his attention between him and the goings on. Then, almost out of character, Albrecht made a quick turn toward Dominique, this time wearing an unmistakable frown, then quickly returned to his papers. Again, Gale was puzzled.

"Mr. Albrecht. Would you care to reiterate plaintiff's position?" asked the judge.

"If it please the court, plaintiff's case will rest primarily on the FAA report in addition to cross-examination of defendant's witnesses," said Albrecht, after which he stole another quick glance at Dominique. "That is, if Your Honor agrees."

"It's fine here, Mr. Albrecht," Judge Rickey replied, then addressed Sam Rader. "Mr. Rader, it's your courtroom."

Gale wanted to stop the proceedings for a moment to confer with Rader if for no other reason than to clue him in on the glances by their adversary to their star witness, but, figuring it would come out soon anyway, he decided against it.

Rader slowly rose to his feet, stepped to the empty jury box, and gazed out the window. He was pensive and professional in his manner. His dress was formal, and it was obvious that he was prepared. He smiled and nodded to the judge as he held up a multi-page document as he addressed the court. "Your Honor, we fully realize that the Federal Aviation Administration has the responsibility of determining the cause of the crash of this particular aircraft, among other things." He waved the report in the air. "And, we also believe that one person's opinion is simply that, especially in this particular case, since there is no evidence to support anything other than opinions. Certainly it's possible—and I stress *possible*—that the inspector's statement about loading errors, may be based on a number of things, some of which could be nonfactual. For, as we know, the aircraft is at the bottom of a very deep ocean and, as we also know, we have yet to be presented with any firsthand knowledge of how the aircraft did, in fact, go down. In fact, Your Honor, we have no proof that a plane is actually missing, let alone one of Bortens's. No one has seen it, and no one has inspected it." Rader paused effectively, then continued.

"So, in this situation, Your Honor, may I suggest that we look very closely at some very relevant historical data? In that regard, sir, we have one witness to call, one witness only. Our intent will be for her to explain the loading procedures of the downed aircraft and how it was loaded that particular day. In addition, we will provide, for the court to consider, historical data on the crew themselves. With your blessing, we shall continue in that direction."

"You may, Mr. Rader." Judge Rickey addressed the plaintiff table. "Mr. Albrecht, do you have any problem with this approach?"

"We concur, Your Honor."

"Mr. Rader. Please continue."

"Thank you. If it please the court, we call Dominique Fabours." Rader turned and motioned for Dominique to take the stand.

Dominique walked past the two tables to the front of the courtroom, where she was sworn in as an expert witness. She took her place in the chair next to the bench. Gale couldn't help but notice her nervousness as she prepared to respond to Rader's questions. Perhaps it was due to the seriousness of her testimony, especially with the loss of the two crewmen's lives. She folded her hands in her lap and leaned forward, ready to participate.

Rader was a gifted orator, and his questions were balanced between professional lingo and everyday common words that prompted Dominique to reply in the same way. He was good at persuading and, as such, was an effective trial lawyer. He would use no notes but, instead, would rely on his natural talents to convince the judge to see it his way. He would simply ask Dominique several questions that he knew she would answer truthfully.

Rader opened, "Miss Fabours, we wish to thank you for taking your time to give this court the benefit of your experience as the operations manager for the Bortens Air Cargo Company. The reason the court is interested in your knowledge and opinions in this matter is because we have no firsthand knowledge of the plane's disappearance. In other words, we have no physical evidence that can prove or disprove that what the FAA purports to be a true accounting of the events on that particular day. What we do have, though, is our reliance on, and the benefit of, your own experience of this particular aircraft's capabilities and those of the crew. May we count on your honest appraisal of the events prior to the crash?"

"Your Honor," Albrecht protested. "Mr. Rader is leading the court. If she answers yes, does that not affirm that all he said was true and now part of the record?"

"Point well taken, Mr. Albrecht," answered the judge. "Is that an objection?"

"Yes sir. We object."

"In that case, objection overruled. I see nothing wrong with the defendant's efforts to set the stage for Miss Fabours as an expert witness. And, her testimony is open for your cross-examination." He gave Albrecht a firm nod and turned to Rader. "Please proceed, Mr. Rader."

Again, Gale watched Albrecht closely and analyzed the last exchange. While Albrecht acknowledged the judge's decision, was something behind that tentative smile of his? Was he pleased with the overruled objection? After all, the better she does, the worse it is for Albrecht. Or was it simply theatrics based on his not having much of a case?

Rader continued, "Miss Fabours, would you please tell the court what your duties are at Bortens?"

"I am the operations manager for Bortens Air Cargo," she testified. "I report to the San Francisco head office, but I work in New York City. We have four aircraft attached to Kennedy International. My primary duties include those of managing all traffic for Bortens."

"Excuse me, Miss Fabours," Judge Rickey interjected. "But would you define what you mean by 'managing all traffic?'"

"Yes." Dominique looked at the judge who returned her smile. "I would be happy to. When we receive instructions from San Francisco that we have cargo to transport, it is my responsibility to make things happen from that point on. I arrange the crew, the fuel, the loading, the documentation, the flight plan, and nearly every other activity necessary to ensure that the cargo arrives safely."

"Would you say then, Miss Fabours, that very few things take place without your knowledge?" asked Rader.

"No sir. I mean, yes sir. They do not."

"Your Honor, if you please, I'd like to dispense with further discussion of Bortens's business operations and Miss Fabours's responsibilities to direct our attention to the loading of the plane in question." Anticipating the judge's response, he turned to Dominique. "Miss Fabours, would you describe what occurred on that particular day?"

"On that day, I was asked specifically to be present during the loading of the cargo."

"And were you physically at the site where that aircraft was loaded on that particular day, Miss Fabours?"

"Yes, I was."

"And could you tell us what happened?"

She cleared her throat and looked at Rader, then Gale, then finally at Albrecht. She had made her decision. "Everything was loaded properly."

Gale watched as Albrecht closed his eyes and his face turned red. The veins in his neck seemed to pulsate as he loosened his tie. Albrecht fidgeted with a pencil, repeatedly tapping it on the legal pad in front of him. Then he scribbled something on the pad.

Gale suspected that Albrecht's mind was elsewhere for a brief moment because he missed the fact that Rader had returned to the defendant's table and the judge had called for his cross-examination. His cold, dark eyes were half closed; his mustache quivered with anger. Suddenly, the pencil he held in both hands splintered, sending pieces flying in all directions. It broke the silence.

Six

"Mr. Albrecht. I said, your witness!"

Regaining control, Albrecht stood and approached the witness stand. Although he held on, he was fuming. "Miss Fabours, I understand you are in charge of operations?"

"Yes, I am."

"Would that include everything associated with the movement of your airplanes? Everything includes gassing them? Checking the oil? Washing the windows? That sort of thing?"

"I have a staff that performs those duties. But, yes, I oversee it."

"Then you manage. You don't work."

Dominique hesitated. "Well, yes, I manage others."

"I can't imagine someone such as yourself physically gassing up the planes, loading them? You know, physically touching the cargo."

Judge Rickey interrupted, "Is that a question, Mr. Albrecht?"

"Excuse me, Your Honor. Miss Fabours, do you physically load the plane?"

Again she hesitated, thinking about her answer carefully before giving it. "It's like I said. I do not do the work myself. The people whom I supervise do those things."

"Then would you say your job is an office job? Is it clerical?"

"In some ways. I'd question the clerical part. I supervise and have quite a few—"

"Miss Fabours, please be specific and answer with a yes or no. Please? Are the bulk of your duties handled in an office? Yes or no?"

Dominique replied, "Yes," then clenched her teeth to keep from saying more.

"Then on the day in question, didn't you then have someone else inspecting the loading of the cargo?"

"No."

"Excuse me. But didn't we understand you to say others performed those direct duties? And not yourself?"

"Normally this is true. But—"

"Miss Fabours, please. A yes or no."

"Would you ask that question again?"

"Did you not say your job was more office and that you supervised others who performed the actual loading and inspecting?" Albrecht pushed. "And, couldn't we all agree that you were physically not present on the day this particular air plane was loaded?"

"Yes. I mean no."

"Now what is it Miss Fabours? Is it a yes or—"

"I object, Your Honor," Rader interrupted. "He's badgering the witness."

"Objection sustained," Judge Rickey responded. "Mr. Albrecht, please give the witness a chance to answer. And keep your questions singular in nature. One question at a time, please."

"Sorry, Your Honor," said Albrecht as he addressed Dominique. "Miss Fabours, again please. Were you there at the time of loading of this particular plane?"

"Yes."

"Your Honor," asked Albrecht. "Could I have a moment?"

"You may. Do you wish the witness to step down?"

Six

"No sir. I'll be only a moment." Albrecht returned to his table and thumbed through a file folder, searching for something and muttering to himself. Then he returned and continued. "Miss Fabours, did you physically inspect the cargo and the tie-downs to which the cargo were attached?"

"Yes."

"Can you tell us, then, the condition of the tie-downs themselves? I mean, what they were made of? When they were installed? Their condition? How they work?"

Remembering to answer directly and briefly, she replied, "They are O-rings welded to the flooring."

"Would you say welded or braised? Are they aluminum or steel, or brass, or copper, or what?"

Dominique stopped and thought. "I would say aluminum."

"OK, then. Aluminum they are. Welded to the floor. Is that correct?"

"Yes. I believe that is correct. But I can't honestly—"

"Ah now, Miss Fabours. Just a simple yes or no. Now tell me how the cargo on this day was actually attached to the tie-downs. Better yet, did you witness the actual tying down?"

"Well I—"

"Miss Fabours."

"Yes," Dominique replied.

"Thank you. With what did they secure the cargo to the tie-downs?"

"Webbed belting," she answered.

"And you actually did the work yourself?"

"No. The crew—"

"Miss Fabours," Albrecht warned. "A yes or no would be sufficient."

"No."

"Then would you please tell the court if you actually saw the tie-down maneuver yourself. I mean, did you see them being tied down? On that day?"

"They always—"

"Yes or no, Miss Fabours."

Dominique hesitated. A tear formed in her eye but she fought it back. She replied, "No."

"Your Honor," said Albrecht. "I move that the court disallow the testimony of this witness as expert. From her own testimony, she is unable to verify that this particular cargo, on this particular day, was tied down in any particular manner, if at all."

Judge Rickey, obviously taken back by Dominique's weak testimony, moved the papers around his desk, looking for a quick and reasonable answer. He nodded at Albrecht in partial agreement, then looked at Rader as if to ask for help. "Gentlemen, here is how the court sees this situation. I see no basis for either side being anything other than completely honest. The expert witness is admittedly a little weak in her testimony of that particular day's happenings. But I believe, too, that just because she did not witness the actual tying down of the cargo does not mean it wasn't tied down properly. In other words, in this case, lacking proof does not mean it did not occur. The scales haven't been tipped to the extent that I concur with the plaintiff's contentions, Mr. Albrecht. On the other hand, I can certainly see how a mistake could have occurred, and lacking evidence

Six

either way, I am unable to draw any other conclusion except one, which would be fair to all. Now, as I say this, don't for a minute feel that either plaintiff or defendant has not had its day in court. Am I understood?"

Both attorneys nodded, and Judge Rickey continued. "Bortens Air Cargo has an exemplary history according to the FAA. I don't see any reason for punitive damages in this case. I don't believe for a minute, Mr. Albrecht, that Bortens meant to do your clients any harm. Flying is a risky business, and I believe that your clients were well aware of the hazards. Look at their backgrounds. It says here that the captain volunteered for four extra tours of duty at Vietnam. Therefore, I'll award and direct that Bortens pay the required sum to the families but, hear me when I say, no punitive damages. Oh, and yes, Mr. Albrecht. No attorney fees either. This case is adjourned. Gentlemen, thank you for your patience in this matter."

SEVEN

"You two go ahead. I'll catch up." Dominique headed for the ladies room as Gale and Rader took the long hallway to the courthouse's front entrance.

For her, it had been a day of mixed feelings. On one hand, she felt good about her testimony and good about the judge's findings for her company. On the other, she felt uneasy, maybe a little anxious, about her run-in with Albrecht the night before. The offer was good, and God knows she needed the money, but the thought of not telling the truth turned her cold. It mattered to her. She valued her job, Rader's friendship, and, above all, her sense of decency.

Her heels clicked against the solid marble floor as she headed for the ladies' room. Both Rader and Gale were out of sight. Although it was midday, the corridor was empty, except for her. A pair of oak benches were the only furnishings, placed on the cold marble floors, halfway between the doors of two courtrooms, which were also empty.

She was so intent on getting to the ladies' room and heading home that she didn't see Albrecht sitting on one of the benches. Without a word, he reached out and grabbed her arm, spinning her around, dead in her tracks. He was too strong for her. He pulled her next to him and held her tightly.

It came to her how foolish she was to think that she would get off this easily. "You're hurting me," she cried.

Albrecht kept a tight grip on his prey. "What the hell were you doing in there? I thought we had a deal."

"Let go. I can explain," she whimpered.

Albrecht held strong as he led her down the vacant corridor to a rear entrance and through a set of double doors, where he forced her down the steps to where a black limo waited at the curb with its engine idling. Albrecht quickly opened the door and forced her into the rear seat, following and slamming the door behind him. The car sped down the alley and made a left onto St. James, heading for the entrance to the Manhattan Bridge.

Meanwhile Gale and Rader were waiting for Dominique on the front sidewalk, about fifty feet from the alley. "What do you think, Sam?" asked Gale as he checked his watch. "She should've been here by now."

"I think I'll have a look. Be right back." Rader walked briskly up the steps and through the courthouse door.

Gale kicked a cigar butt into the gutter as a black limo spun out of the alley, switched to the far left lane, and hung a left at the next corner. Before it made the turn, for some unexplained reason, Gale spotted the wet tire on the right rear side which, since it hadn't rained since he'd been here, he thought was unusual.

Across Foley Square, he recognized the Municipal Building, and a little beyond that, the Police Plaza. He figured the limo was heading in that direction but gave it no further thought. He replayed the earlier situation between Albrecht-Dominique and concluded that he had no idea of whatever relationship may have existed then, now, or anytime. So where was she, he wondered?

Rader hurried down the steps, and when he reached the sidewalk, looked frantically from side to side, obviously concerned. "She's not in there."

Gale's anxiety increased. "Maybe she—"

"I don't know Bill. I'm not sure. It's not like her to just leave."

"But this is her town. Hell, maybe she caught a cab and went home."

"Nope. She didn't catch a cab. It's lunch time, and that's where we were supposed to be headed. No, I tell you, Bill, something's wrong."

Gale shared Rader's concern, and although he hadn't known her for any length of time, he thought it odd that she'd leave without saying anything. He thought for a minute and then pointed to the front of the courthouse and said, "You take the front. I'll meet you on the other side."

Rader ran toward the front of the courthouse as Gale jogged down the alley. As he neared the rear steps, he noticed a puddle of water at the curb. Some of it had splashed over the curb, onto the sidewalk, not far from the steps leading to the rear door. The tire tracks leading from the puddle were too much of a coincidence.

He stopped at the top of the steps before opening the doors to see if Rader was headed his way. He poked his head inside and, with the door half open, verified that it was the way to Rickey's courtroom. Rader had just rounded the corner and was heading his way.

"This is where it happened, Sam." He held the door open and pointed toward the street. "She got into a car right there."

"How can you tell?" Rader asked.

"Look at this. She came down the steps there." He motioned from the door to the sidewalk. "The car must have been waiting because she got in right there. And I'll tell you what. I don't think it was voluntary on her part." He kneeled and touched a fresh scrape in the concrete. "She was wearing high heels wasn't she?"

"I think so. Why? Does it look like—"

"Yup. These are scuff marks. Damn it all!" Gale snapped his finger as he thought about the speeding limo with the wet tire. "I'll be damned."

"So, you think she was kidnapped?"

"I think so. Come on." Gale led Rader down the alley to the street, following the same course he knew the car had taken. "I think it went down the alley, turned right, went by us, then took another left." He pointed to where he had been standing earlier. "Right in front of me, a quick turn and presto, it was gone."

Rader walked to the curb and looked both ways, where he agreed. "Doesn't make sense."

"I'm afraid I have to agree." He gave Rader an inquisitive look.

"So what's next?" Rader asked. "I've a plane to catch in the morning, but I can cancel it if you want me to hang around."

"I don't think so, but wait," Gale muttered. He traced what he thought might have been her last few moments prior to her abduction. He hustled to the corner and studied the streets, looking toward the Manhattan Bridge and Brooklyn off in the distance. "That's it." He turned to face Rader. There was a twinkle in his eye and a sound of danger in his voice. "They've got her."

"Who?" asked Rader, taken back by the investigator's findings.

"Albrecht. There's something fishy going on between her and that sneaky son of a bitch. I can feel it in my bones." Gale had no intention of letting on that he had any suspicion of Dominique being connected to Albrecht. He couldn't put his finger on it, but Albrecht was more than upset at the judge's decision. But then, his attack on cross-examination was terrible, so he had no one to blame but himself. But why should the man be so upset at Dominique simply telling it like it happened? He asked Rader, "How's our budget?" There was a sense of urgency in his question.

Rader gave Gale an appraising look. "I don't think it's a question of money. It's a question of her safety. What do you need from me?"

"Nothing." Gale shook Rader's hand, then signaled a cab. "You play it cool, and I'll be in touch."

* * * * * * * * * *

Bayville is a small town on the north shore of Long Island. Across the sound from Stamford, Connecticut, it isn't that far from New York City. It's quiet during the winter and very peaceful. When it rains, the water in the sound is as smooth as glass. When it blows, the water gets choppy and small boat warnings fly on every marina.

During spring break, it was a far different place. The town became instantly alive, crawling with young coeds and their fun-seeking boyfriends, anxious for a quickie on the sand. Topless parties were the norm as young kids hopped from one party to the next, all with one thing in mind. But for now, it was a cozy, little hamlet by the bay.

The oily smell of the small outboards permeated the foggy air as their small wakes rose and fell beneath a pair of gulls paddling between a row of floating homes.

The limo stopped in a reserved parking space next to the Bayville Marina sign. Albrecht pulled Dominique from the car and slammed the door shut. As he pushed her, she staggered down a pair of two-by-sixes that served as the gangway to the planked walkway running parallel to the shore. He forced her onto the second walkway and pushed her toward the end.

Next to the end unit floated a weather-beaten house built in the early forties. It was a single-story structure with an equally weather-beaten roof. A metal chimney poked from the middle of the roof. A rusty wind deflector squeaked as the wind pushed it one way and then the next.

Since there was no need to push her any farther, Albrecht released his grip, and they stepped inside. Like being hit in the face by a musty blanket, the place had a stench like a stale locker room. The rug was damp from months of not having any heat or fresh air to help dry out the moisture that had permeated the shanty's thin walls. Albrecht locked the door and turned the thermostat to seventy. "This is home, baby."

Afraid to sit on any of the stained furniture or breathe the noxious odor, Dominique held her breath as she studied Albrecht and the interior of the room and decided both were sleazy. In one corner was a cracked vase containing a dead plant. A smelly sofa and matching love seat were the only attempt at furnishings. At the first sign of warmth, she finally breathed and looked at him in disgust. "What are you going to do with me?"

"You, my dear, are going to cooperate with me. You failed me today, miserably too. And we can't allow that." Albrecht took one of the folding chairs that was facing the table, turned it around, and sat down, elbows on the back of the chair, palms holding his chin. "You're going to wish you'd done as you'd promised."

"But it's all over. Court is over. And I didn't lie for you and that's final." She had an air of completeness about her.

"Oh no. That's where you are wrong, my dear." He stood up, legs still straddling the chair. His arms were outstretched and his smile was wicked. "You see, we've just begun. We've only just begun."

Dominique ran toward the door, but Albrecht got there first. He caught her by the arm and spun her around, knocking her to the floor. He followed her down and pounced on top, knocking the breath out of her. She tried to slap him, but his well-seasoned street fighting days had taught him all the defensive moves.

He held her wrists firmly. "Don't even try it. You're no match, and I've a good mind to toss you in the bay."

He pushed her hand to her face, causing the stem of her watch to scratch her forehead, which started to bleed slightly. She sobbed quietly in the strong hold of her captor. Albrecht seemed to thrive on this kind of action. He loved control.

"Are you ready to listen now?" he asked as he loosened his grip and rose to stand over her, one foot on each side of her slender waist.

She continued to sob and touched her forehead with her finger. She pulled it away with a touch of blood on it. The bleeding had nearly stopped. The wound wasn't serious, but she was still frightened. She felt he was capable of much more, and, because she wasn't interested in learning the hard way, she thought she'd play along with it since it beat the alternative. "OK. But can I get up?"

Holding his position, he grinned. After a second, he stepped away, allowing her to stand.

"Do you have any tissue?" she sobbed.

"Above the sink," he replied.

She took a damp tissue from an old, flowered cardboard facial tissue box. She wanted to wet it but was afraid of what might come out of the faucet. She licked it and dabbed at her forehead. She tucked her blouse into her skirt while attempted to rearrange herself. "What can I do now?"

He sat back in the folding chair and rocked forward, beating a steady rhythm with his right hand on the metal seat. He returned the chair back to all fours and sat straight. "Now we're getting somewhere. You're going to call the judge and read this." He handed her a piece of paper on which was neatly typed a few sentences.

She leaned against the kitchen window and read the note. She sighed and shook her head, then let her arms fall to her side, holding the note with one hand. She looked out the window and saw a mother duck and her ducklings waddle across the slippery, weathered deck; upon reaching the edge, the ducklings followed their mother into the smooth water between the floating homes, paddling to a floating deadhead. She stared at Albrecht. She was disturbed and angry but had no other option than to play it out as far as she could. "How about the money?"

"The same deal stands," replied Albrecht. "You'll get the money, just as I promised. But you may wish to bear in mind, my dear, we're not always so polite. But then, we're not all that bad either."

"What makes you think I need the money?" she asked.

Albrecht handed her an envelope that had been opened and its contents obviously read. It was addressed to Dominique at her Village apartment. It was from the Sunrise Mental Care Center, a name with which she had been very familiar over the years. She opened it and read it silently, and began to weep. She replaced the letter inside the envelope, folded it, and held it to her chest. Without looking at Albrecht she asked, "Where's the phone?"

"Not so fast. We'll wait till tomorrow. We want to give you time to think this over, you know. We can't rush it."

Her heart sunk after reading the letter, and even more when she realized she'd be spending the night here. Albrecht showed her to the only bedroom in the musty quarters, then went back to the living room. It was small and dimly lit, and the end tables and window sill were coated with dust. A thin coating of moisture covered the only window in the small bedroom. She thought of getting a message to someone on the outside. She touched her index finger to the window. The cool water trickled down her finger. She peered through the fresh clearing made by hastily sliding her finger across the wet surface, spelling "Go for Help," but only the windowless side of another floating home was her view. She decided it was no use and got back in touch with her reality for the moment. There was no other alternative than to ride it out and hope for the best. She sat there for hours staring into space; finally darkness came. The sheets were cold and damp, but, surprisingly, she quickly fell asleep.

EIGHT

Dominique woke suddenly to find Albrecht standing at the foot of her bed, hands at his side; in one hand he held a butcher knife. She had no idea how long he had been there. She looked up at him with questioning eyes. The fear that had been with her the evening before had suddenly returned. She pulled the covers around her neck to hide from his cold stare as she fumbled for something to say.

"How long—"

"Get up," Albrecht interrupted. "You have an important call to make." He motioned with his knife hand toward a door next to the closet. "The shower's in there. Don't think of escaping because there's no way out." He walked out of the bedroom, then turned. "You can scream all you want. There's nobody around to hear you."

The hot shower was a warm relief from the tensions she'd been feeling since she'd been kidnapped the day before. She shuddered at the thought of what damage the knife could do.

She wept for her sister, whom she had taken care of throughout their school years. The thought of the two of them playing as children added some strength, but she feared not enough to help her through all of this ordeal. Willamina was older, but mentally, she was still a child. The letter was clear, and it was painful. Willamina would be transferred to a state institution unless, by some stroke of luck, a bunch of money fell from the sky. How she dreaded the thought of her sister being all but forgotten in a state institution. The state-run facilities were cold and impersonal. She shuddered at the thought of it, and remembered the knife.

Because Willamina's condition required constant care, plus the fact that Dominique loved her so, her senses of right and wrong were now being tested. To save her sister from a state institution, Fabours saw no other options. And, the cold realization that her own life was in danger made it very clear to her. With the threat of Albrecht's knife a reality, she picked up the phone.

"Judge Rickey? Judge Thomas Rickey?" Dominique asked. "Sir, this is Dominique Fabours. I was in your court-room with Bortens Air Cargo." A cold chill came over her, but she persisted, influenced by the fear of seeing Willamina in a dingy state mental hospital. "I have something I wish to say to you. It's very difficult, but I must say it. In court yes-terday, I testified that the cargo was tied down properly." She cleared her throat. "What I mean to say is that I may have been wrong. I wasn't sure. But now that I've gotten away, out here to Bayville, the sea air is clearing my head, and I'm thinking that I can't really say for certain. But I'm afraid I may have misrepresented what actually happened."

Eight

As Albrecht relaxed his stance and lowered the knife, she breathed easier, and waited for a response.

Finally the judge said, "Young lady, are you saying that you falsified your testimony?"

Again, the cold chill swept through her. "But Mr. Rickey, I mean Your Honor, I didn't mean to—"

The judge's voice was strong. "Miss Fabours. Please think about what you are saying. You were the only witness in this case. It was your testimony that became the basis for my decision. Are you sure of what you are saying?"

Gazing through the window, she saw herself pushing her sister on a swing at the playground. Then the image faded as she focused on a passing sailboat. "Yes sir, I am." She continued her lie. "I can't live with myself, knowing I lied to you and maybe caused more grief to the families of our crew. I'm sorry. Well, I didn't really lie. What I mean is I was just mistaken and had no idea that the outcome—"

"Well, young lady, you had me fooled. My clerk will be in touch with you soon. Is that understood?"

"Yes, sir, it is. I'm so very sorry."

The stern of the sailboat had disappeared behind a large yacht when she hung up. She felt vacant but also relieved that the knife was no longer an instant threat.

* * * * * * * * * *

Gale signed for breakfast, then entered the lobby. As he walked past the front desk, the attractive blond behind the reservation desk held up a note and called his name. He read the note and hurried to Rader's room.

Rader hung up the phone and poured two cups of coffee from a room service carafe. He handed one to Gale. "Bill, we're in a heap of trouble."

"What are you talking about?" Gale asked as he sat on the edge of the bed, warming his hands with the cup of hot coffee. "Did you locate Dominique?"

"Not exactly," Rader said, shaking his head in disbelief. "You're not going to believe it, but that was Judge Rickey."

"Hold it. You're going way too fast. Do you know where Dominique is? And what's the judge got to do with it?"

"Rickey said that Dominique had called him, this morning for all I know. Come to think of it, it must have been this morning. He was furious. He said that Dominique confessed that she'd lied about her testimony and was recanting it."

"What are you talking about?" Gale asked.

"I don't know. He wants to see me."

"Like—"

"Like now," Rader interrupted. "I booked a later flight."

Gale stopped for a minute and thought about where Dominique may have gone. "Did he give you any clue about where she was? Anything?"

"Nothing, except she was calling long distance."

"Long distance?" Gale asked. "How would he know unless she said something? With today's phones, you could call from the other side of the world and it would sound like you're in the next room."

"You want to pick his brain?" Rader asked.

"No," Gale responded. His thoughts were back on the limo with the wet tires. "She must be somewhere on Long Island."

Eight

"How do you figure?"

"Just a hunch, but I'll fill you in later," Gale said as he replayed the image of the limo making the left turn, thinking that the driver's choices were few, except for Long Island. "OK, you talk to the judge, and I'll find Dominique. Here's my cell number." He wrote the number on a hotel note pad and handed it to Rader. "Call me with anything you get. I'm out of here."

With Rader on the way to the courthouse, Gale drove the rented car across the Manhattan Bridge onto Long Island where, guided by his instincts, he decided on the sound side of the island rather than the ocean side. He turned north from the main highway and picked several small roads leading to the waterfront. None panned out. He found no traces of the limo. He scoured the streets, back roads, and parking lots in every village close to the water's edge, and still he found nothing. Then the cell phone rang.

"Sam? Is that you?"

"Bill. I'm here with Judge Rickey. There seems to be more to it. The judge said that Dominique sounded nervous and uncertain." Rader paused, then got back on the line. "Well, here. Just a second—"

"Mr. Gale, this is Tom Rickey," the judge introduced himself. "Mr. Rader felt I should tell you firsthand. Are you there?"

"Yes, Your Honor. Please go on."

"Miss Fabours sounded frightened but in some mysterious way, she also sounded sure of herself, like she may have been trying to say more but couldn't. I feel I agree with Mr. Rader that there's more to it. Therefore, I'll allow you forty-eight hours to find her and clarify the situation. I understand she may be missing. Is that correct?"

"Yes, it is," Gale replied. "I stopped by her apartment last night, and she hadn't been there. I waited for a couple of hours, but I doubt very much if she showed up at all. I don't think there's any question. She's been kidnapped, Your Honor. Could you tell anything from her voice? Were there any familiar sounds, like in the background?"

"Yes, there were, as a matter of fact," the judge replied. "Perhaps a television, tuned to a cartoon show even. I heard a quacking sound. Ducks. And I seem to remember her mentioning Bayville. I think it may be on Long Island."

"Hold it," Gale said as he fumbled through the glove box for a map. "Here's one. Hold on for a second. OK, here it is. Bayville. It's on the map, and I'm pretty close. I'm going to try it. Forty-eight hours, you say?"

"Yes. Based on what she said, we have a potential perjury situation here. But I am inclined to agree with Mr. Rader that something else is involved too. Keep in touch. Here's Mr. Rader."

"What do you think? Could she be—"

"Hate to be rude, but I've got to go. I'll get back to you."

Bayville was a small village—small enough that the limo would be spotted easily. And sure enough, there it was, parked under the Bayville Marina sign. It was one of only a few cars parked in the lot. Seeing that the limo was empty, he drove slowly through the parking lot, adjacent to the water's edge, surveying every houseboat and every floating walkway. Nothing appeared suspicious. He was sure Dominique was in one of them. But which one? He parked behind an old grocery store next to the parking lot and walked across the gravel lot and down the gangway onto the floating walkway that ran parallel to the shore.

Gale figured that there must be at least a hundred houseboats secured to the finger piers that were leading perpendicular from the main walkway. Stepping onto the first pier, he noticed the ducklings following the quacking commands of their mother as they waddled along the pier. The mother duck slipped silently into the water to retrieve a straggler and bring it safely back. Slowly he crouched and placed his palm on the window of the first houseboat to feel for heat or any other signs of life. He repeated this for the next two houses until on the fourth, he felt the warmth from the inside heat, then withdrew quietly.

A narrow platform ran between the houseboats, Gale guessed, to give the owners something to stand on while painting or making repairs. Trusting his weight wouldn't tip the narrow floating structure, he put first one foot then the other onto the walkway. It held steady as he crawled to the first window and slowly raised his head. Through the partially fogged window, he saw an unmade bed, with a pair of women's shoes at its side. As he stretched higher to get a better look, his foot slipped on the algae-covered boards. He broke his fall by grabbing the windowsill and holding himself steady.

He rested for a few seconds to see if his presence had been discovered and, deciding it hadn't been, continued inching his way to a second window. By its size, he guessed it to be the living room's. He pressed his ear against the wall. He heard two muffled voices, one a woman's and the other a man's. He crept closer to the large window, where he slowly raised his head and peered inside. A dirty curtain made for a hazy view of the room. He moved farther to get a clearer view, being careful not to make a sound. There he was. Albrecht sat on the living room sofa, but Gale couldn't see Dominique. Then, he heard her voice.

He ducked to avoid being detected, even by her. He wasn't sure of her reaction, so it was better to play it safe. He studied the slippery walkway as he continued toward the rear of the floating home. At this point, he realized he couldn't possibly reach the deck without endangering his mission. He had reached the end of one window only to find another, this time one that extended closer to the floor. Even sliding on his stomach, he would chance being seen from the inside. At this point, his choices were slim to nonexistent. If he continued, he would surely be spotted. If he returned to the front and broke down the door, he couldn't be sure of Albrecht's position. Besides, the time period between breaking down the door and reaching Albrecht would put him at a disadvantage.

He lunged past the window and fell onto the rear sun deck. Had it not been for the railing, his momentum would certainly have carried him beyond the deck and into the sound's frigid waters. Albrecht saw him and jumped to the door, throwing it open, breaking the door's window and spraying glass onto the deck. Albrecht was on him in a split second, knife in one hand. As Gale pushed himself up from the railing, he took Albrecht's foot in the stomach with full force. It knocked the wind out of him, and he fell to the deck. Albrecht recoiled and tried the knife one more time, but Gale rolled over as Albrecht struck and missed, losing his balance long enough for Gale to strike with both powerful legs. Like a pair of industrial strength shears, he closed them on both of Albrecht's knees, toppling him to the deck in agonizing pain. Like lightning, Gale was on top of him with a knee thrust into the small of the wicked attorney's back. At that time, he couldn't see the knife but knew it was still a threat. But Albrecht was too wiry—he rolled through the sliding door and onto the deck, scrambling for the water, as Gale literally flew through the door, landing full force on top of the attorney. But it was too late. The small, more agile man slipped from under Gale's bulk and disappeared under the cold, dark water, leaving a small pool of blood on the wet deck.

Stunned by Albrecht's escape, and even more so by the blood he left behind, Gale turned to see Dominique cowering in the kitchen, shaking from fright at what had occurred between the two men. He ran to her and took her into his muscular arms.

Suddenly, the sun deck window shattered and the room filled with fire. Dominique was knocked unconscious by the blast. Instinctively, he crawled down a hallway to where he calculated the front door would be, dragging her with him. In the instant he opened the door, another explosion ripped through the houseboat from behind him. With little choice, he pulled Dominique from the burning building onto the floating walkway. The rotten wood of the old houseboat was excellent fuel for the intense fire, its flames shooting fifty feet into the otherwise peaceful, salty air.

He placed her limp body in the back seat of the rental car, while he quickly scanned the area for Albrecht. His body pumping adrenaline, he was ready for action. But as high as he was and as badly as he wanted the attorney, Dominique needed him far more. She lay motionless. He placed his ear next to her mouth and heard faint breathing, but she lay unconscious.

With limited resources, he held her in one arm while gently pushing her hair away from her closed eyes. He ran his fingers through her shiny black hair and gently massaged her forehead, running his fingers down the bridge of her nose to her cheeks where he wiped away the filth from the explosion. She was beautiful, even as she lay motionless. He patted her gently on both cheeks until finally her eyes opened halfway. A weak smile formed, and she again closed her eyes. Tears formed, but her smile remained. Her chest rose slightly then fell again as she took in a series of deep breaths. He was concerned that she might have a concussion or other internal injuries.

Slowly, she opened her eyes again, and tried to blink away the tears which, by now, were streaming from her beautiful green eyes, flowing down her delicate cheeks.

"Are you OK? Are you hurt?" he asked.

She took a few moments to attempt an assessment, then she responded. "I don't feel any broken bones, and I think I'm OK. What happened? "Where's Albrecht?"

"Let's just say he's not going to bother you for a while. There was an explosion. The houseboat caught on fire and somehow, magically, we got out."

"An explosion?" She stopped for a second. "I think I remember now. Yes, I remember everything coming apart and then, that's all."

"Well, you've been through quite a bit. When you're able, you can tell me about it."

* * * * * * * * * *

Less than a hundred feet away, Jopaq hung up the receiver and left the phone booth, rounding the corner of the grocery store, in a hurry to return to the city.

* * * * * * * * * *

Gale's pace had still not slowed, except to care for Dominique. The explosion had to be from an outside source. It was impossible for the place to have been wired because both of them were still inside when the place blew. The realization that they were being followed still hung with him. But who would want Dominique out of the way? Maybe it was meant for Albrecht?

He grabbed his cell phone and dialed the judge's private chambers. "Hello, Judge Rickey; Bill Gale here. Just wanted you to know that Miss Fabours is safe, and that I'll be in touch as soon as I can put all this together." Rather than give the judge any time to respond, he finished his conversation as quickly as he began it. "I suspect this matter goes much further than any of us realized. I'll phone you when I have more information."

On their drive back to Manhattan, Dominique sat in silence for a while, and then her memory started to return. "Oh, Mr. Gale, it was awful. He grabbed me right after court and took me to that terrible place. He told me that if I didn't recant my testimony, something terrible would happen. So, I called Judge Rickey and lied to him, telling him that I had actually lied in court and that it was really Bortens's fault after all. Oh, Mr. Gale, I feel terrible."

"We'll get to the bottom of it soon. Right now, let's get you back to a comfortable place to stay. I don't want you going home."

"Who do you think is trying to kill me?" she asked.

"I'm not sure it's you they're after," Gale replied, still replaying the previous events. "Not sure at all."

Crossing the Brooklyn Bridge, the enormous harbor was choked with ships at anchor, awaiting their turn to dock and unload their cargo. Gale picked the Regent Park Hotel because it was close and probably more, because its name was similar to the Regency, where he'd checked in with Rader. Being north of the Village, it was also close to Dominique's place. Just the ticket to get out of harm's way.

As he pulled to the curb, the left side-view mirror shattered as one of Jopaq's silent bullets came too close for comfort. Gale pushed Dominique out the passenger door, and they both ran for cover between two parked cars. Gale raised his head above the trunk of one of the cars; he saw nothing but figured it wasn't the time to stay in one spot. Rather than giving away their new location to whoever was after them, Gale grabbed Dominique's hand and rushed across the street and down the stairway into the subway station, where they caught the first train to Battery Park.

The deafening screech of metal against metal made him cringe as the aging subway strained to navigate the quick turn into Battery Park Station. He closed his eyes for a second and gritted his teeth. It was like fingernails on a blackboard. Once into daylight, he felt they hadn't been followed. But just in case they had, it was time to narrow the odds a bit. At least if they boarded the boat to the Statue of Liberty, he could watch every person came on board. If they weren't followed, he'd have the time to get to know her better, and find out what was going on with her abduction and now these attempts on their lives.

When they reached the island, the deckhand made a perfect toss to the cleat, and the stern line stretched tight. The boat lurched to a stop and a man fell against him, forcing him even tighter against the railing. Instinctively, Gale pushed back, knocking the smaller man against the cabin's bulkhead. As Gale was about to apologize, the man quickly continued along his way toward the gangway, without saying a word.

* * * * * * * * *

Jopaq feared that he'd been recognized. If so, it was a mistake that he had been well trained to avoid making. How could he have been so foolish? So clumsy? He nudged his elbow against his right side to ensure that the automatic was still in place, its silencer efficiently attached. He again waited for the right opportunity.

* * * * * * * * *

Looming above the island, the statue was a wonderful sight. It was tall and majestic, but Gale had no time to revisit Americana. The two walked to a park bench overlooking the water, where they sat quietly for a few seconds, until Gale began talking. "What happened back there?"

Before Dominique had time to answer, Gale noticed him—the same guy who bumped into him on the boat. As Gale watched the little man enter the base of the statue, he quickly escorted Dominique back to the boat, which was already pulling away from the dock. Gale leaped over the increasingly larger span of water onto the boat's stern, pulling Dominique with him. The rude man was not in sight.

Back ashore, Battery Park was teeming with excitement. The lines to the boats were long, and those who weren't in one of them were walking along the shoreline or sitting on one of many park benches, enjoying the view. Kids were busy with their in-line skates and skateboards, in clear defiance of the signs. A dog leaped into the air to catch a Frisbee, then just stood there, tail wagging furiously, happy to have pleased his master but undecided as to what he should do next.

They found a park bench, as Gale resumed his inquiry. "Well, do you want to talk about it?" he asked.

"Yes. Yes, I do. I'll tell you everything."

"OK," he responded.

She took a deep breath and began. "I was wrong to do what I did. I mean I was wrong to get caught up with that guy."

"You mean Albrecht?"

"Yes. You see, I admit that I need the money, but not to the extent that I would ever lie in court, or place anyone in danger."

"What money?" Gale asked.

Eight

"Albrecht offered me a large sum of money to recant my testimony." She replied.

"So that's what it's all about—money," said Gale.

"I'll explain," replied Dominique. "I have a sister who is autistic. She needs constant attention. Our folks are gone and, well, I'm all she has. And, honestly, it's quite a chore."

"You mean the responsibility?" Gale asked.

"Not so much the responsibility," she replied. "More, the worry. She's really OK where she is, and all that. That's not it. It's, well, it's very expensive."

"Are you responsible for her?"

"Yes and no. She receives disability from Social Security, and the state is providing some help too. But she still depends on me."

"For?"

"For support. All of it. I pay for everything. That is, everything not covered by the two agencies. What I mean by that is...ah...it's a private home."

"Why a private home? The state has homes, don't they?"

"Yes, but I can't see her going to one of them. They're terrible. So, anyway, she's in this private home, and it's very expensive. Not only that, but they've just notified me that the cost is going up, and I must respond or she reverts back to the state and one of their institutions."

"I thought you said it would be a home."

"It is, but it's more like an institution. And, I just can't have that. You understand, don't you?"

"I think I do."

"At first, I thought this might be an opportunity to help my sister. But not really."

"How so?" Gale inquired.

"When the other attorney first approached me, outside my home that night, I nearly allowed my ethics to fly out the window. For a short while, I put my sister's care in front of, let's say, doing what was right. You must think I'm terrible. I wonder what Sam thinks."

"The important thing, though, is that you stood up for yourself," answered Gale. "And I have a sneaking hunch that Sam will understand. After it's all straightened out, I mean."

"I hope so," Dominique pleaded.

"So, what really happened the day of the plane crash?" Gale asked.

Her look was earnest, and her voice was positive but soft. "My first testimony was correct. Everything was loaded properly. As to why the plane went down, I simply don't know. I feel so badly for everyone, but I don't know what caused it. I just don't."

"It's probably safe now," said Gale as he stood to catch a better view of a boat returning to its dock. "But just to be on the safe side, hurry to that deli across the square. I'll meet you there in a few minutes."

As she headed for the deli, Gale doubled back to a spot next to a tree, where he watched the passengers disembark. There he was. The same man who nudged him on the boat. Gale had a strong hunch that he was the man who had been following them. Probably the same one responsible for the explosion too. The man took another path that led away from the street where the deli was located; when it was clear, Gale continued to the street and crossed through heavy traffic to the other side, where he entered the deli. He saw no sign of the small, rude man.

* * * * * * * * * *

Across from the park, in a smoke shop on Whitehall Street, Jopaq watched as Gale and Dominique left the deli. He waited until his targets caught the first available taxi. Hurriedly, Jopaq caught one and followed.

* * * * * * * * * *

Gale gave the driver directions to the Regent Park. The cab took off toward Broadway, then uptown via the Avenue of the Americas. He ducked in and out of traffic and was making good time until, suddenly, the rear window shattered, spraying glass throughout the interior of the cab. The driver's head smashed against the steering wheel, splattering blood onto the windshield and dashboard. The cab careened violently to the right, smashing into a parked car. Chunks of metal and glass flew through the air as Gale forced open the passenger-side door. Frantically, he and Dominique squeezed between the door and the side of the damaged, parked car and onto the street. They hit the sidewalk running. They headed for cover, but there wasn't any. The only way out was around the corner and down the steps into another subway station. Neither looked at the train's destination, and neither much cared. Once the doors closed, Gale quickly scanned the car. No one seemed out of place, and no one seemed to care that the two of them were scared to death and out of breath.

It was a Harlem train. Thankfully, one of its stops was Times Square. They got off and went down one flight and caught the Battery Park going south. They took the Broadway exit and walked a few blocks north, across Washington Square, to the hotel, where he registered the two as Mr. and Mrs. Gale.

He sent Dominique to the room while he stayed in the lobby, watching. After a few minutes, when he was sure they hadn't been followed, he rode the elevator to their room.

It was small but adequate. One window's view was the fire escape, the back alley, and its contents—a cluster of dumpsters. It was getting dark. He checked his watch and realized the day was nearly gone. The shower was running and the door was partially open. He poured himself a glass of water and leaned against the window. He sipped from the half-empty glass and stared through the window, not really caring what was outside. He was in deep thought about the cab driver and their narrow escape. He knew Dominique was somebody's target. At this point, though, he didn't have a clue who that somebody was. The bathroom door opened, and she was wrapped in one of the hotel robes. Even in that, she looked lovely.

NINE

Gale woke to the smell of freshly brewed coffee. She was up, dressed, and ready to go. She placed a coffee mug on a table at the far end of the small room and gave him a knowing smile.

He wanted so much to believe what Dominique had told him the day before, but other things were bugging him. By this time, she had sat on the bed facing him. He looked squarely into her eyes. "I believe your story. But I also need to find some answers." He rose, approached her, and took her hand in his. "I want you to stay here. Don't open the door for anyone. Got it?"

"But where are you going?" she asked.

"I'll be back in a few hours," Gale replied. "I hate to sound like a worn-out television script, but the less you know, the better." Without further words, he was out the door, on the lookout for whomever it was who was after Dominique.

He made it without incident to the Federal Aviation Administration, where he and Dale Wilson went over the report in detail. Nothing within it contained the slightest clue as to the cause of the crash.

"Mr. Gale, I simply can't tell you anything except that until we have retrieved the plane and have proof, we have no choice but to call it a case of pilot error."

Gale caught what may have been a slip. "Is that a plan? I mean, retrieving the plane?"

Wilson backpedaled. "Well, it's been suggested—"

"By whom and how soon?" Gale interrupted.

More backpedaling, Wilson stammered, "Well, you see, it's rather out of the ordinary. I mean, the plane is in deep water, off the shelf, and I doubt really if it's an option."

There was no question in Gale's mind, now, that Wilson knew more than he was letting on. Someone was pulling his chain. "Let me ask you, off the record, OK? How big is this thing, anyway? I mean, how far does this thing go? Why all the bureaucratic smoke screen?"

Still, more backpedaling. "I'm afraid I've given you the wrong impression, Mr. Gale. There's no one interested, besides us that is, in getting to the bottom of it all. Since there's a lawsuit pending, and we're supposed to be the experts, we're really on the spot you know."

"How?"

"We're supposed to have all the answers, as pertains to the cause of the crash. And so forth."

"So forth?" questioned Gale.

"I mean, the cause of the crash, period." Wilson was now finished with the interview. He closed the manila folder, then scribbled something on a piece of paper.

"Is that it?" Gale asked, presuming Wilson's reply.

"Yes," Wilson responded. "That's it."

As Gale stood to leave, he sensed that Wilson was on the verge of wanting to say more, but couldn't. He paused, allowing Wilson a second to continue, but he shrugged his shoulders and remained silent. Wilson turned and moved toward the door as though their meeting was over.

Upon reaching it, however, Wilson paused, turned his head slightly, cleared his throat, and handed Gale the piece of paper. Silently, Gale took it, nodded in agreement and left.

Following the instructions scribbled on the paper, at precisely noon, Gale walked to the Federal Reserve Bank, where, if the directions were correct, he'd meet with Wilson to learn the truth about what was going on behind the scenes. A few minutes passed and no Wilson. After a half-hour, he knew something was wrong, so he hustled back to Wilson's FAA office.

As he neared the elevators, two police officers were rushing from the elevator. He got in and touched the button for Wilson's floor. When the door opened, several people, including two men in suits and two paramedics, were scampering about the office, tending to someone's immediate needs. He shoved his way into Wilson's office to see a gray blanket covering a body lying on the floor behind Wilson's desk. A paramedic confirmed that the body was that of Wilson.

"Mind if I have a look?" Asked Gale. Without waiting for a reply, he stooped down, peeled back the blanket enough to reveal the ashen face of a very dead Mr. Wilson. Blood still oozed from a clean, 9 mm bullet to the right temple. A professional hit, thought Gale.

Gale's thoughts went rampant. Just when he was about to receive what he thought would be a lead in a mysterious puzzle, its provider was out of the picture. His mind raced from Wilson to the plane crash and back to Wilson again. Nothing made sense.

Gale drove back to the Regent Park, where he parked the car in the garage and took the elevator to his floor. As he inserted the key, he noticed a peculiar set of movements next door. A guest had closed the door and was walking to the exit door beyond the elevators, in a hurry. Slowly, Gale withdrew the key. As he did, the lock mechanism made a clicking sound, followed by a muted buzz. He'd heard that noise before, and it meant trouble. Instantly, he threw himself to the side as the door exploded into the hall, embedding wood and metal fragments into the opposite wall.

Gale jumped to his feet and ran through the door, searching for Dominique while hoping for a miracle. To his relief, the room was bare. He ran to the stairwell door just as the elevator door opened, revealing a startled Dominique. He motioned for her to follow, then stopped at the door opening, listening for a sound that would give them a clue which way to go. He figured down, so they quickly descended to the basement and cracked the door leading from the stairwell into the basement area. The corridor was poorly lit and, as far as they could tell, deserted. They listened for a moment and hearing nothing; they entered and cautiously closed the door behind them.

Most of the doors off the main corridor were locked. The unlocked ones turned out to be storage areas for retail tenants on the street level. Coming to the end, they peered around the corner. It turned right. They pulled back. They heard the sound of approaching footsteps echoing in the dark hallway.

Fearing for Dominique's safety, Gale rushed her back toward a single elevator that would take them quickly upstairs and to safety. There wasn't much time, and the footsteps were getting louder and closer. He knew they wouldn't make it to the elevator. Frantically, they began trying the doors along the way. None were open.

Finally, they discovered one that was. Quickly they entered it, pulled the door closed behind them, and waited in silence. They held their breath as the footsteps came closer. Gale had no idea if the intruder had seen or heard them. Had Dominique not been with him, he would've challenged the stranger, but her safety was foremost on his mind. The footsteps passed.

Venturing from the room, they neither saw nor heard a soul. Gale led Dominique along the corridor where they came to another door. It was unlocked, so they pushed it open and entered the hotel's parking structure. A red light marked the entrance to the stairwell that took them up a flight to the sidewalk, where they caught a cab.

He took her to the Regency, his hotel, where he quickly changed into jeans and a dark jacket and left, giving Dominique instructions to stay put and keep the door locked.

TEN

The OILCO building overlooked the East River. At the foot of 49th Street, a block from the United Nations, it housed the headquarters for Oil Explorations, which, in reality, was the private office of Prince Anini before his untimely death. King Saud's special man, Ahmed Persad, a replacement consular to handle pending affairs, now occupied it. The king had gotten wind of the shipment and, although he was troubled at his late brother's decision to handle it alone, he was actually in favor of the idea. They had, in fact, discussed it several times, but, in all reality, the king hadn't taken the time to explore it further. If he had, he no doubt would have put his brother in charge.

A slightly overweight, dark man with coal black hair and horn-rimmed spectacles, Persad's trip was twofold, first to handle the particulars of shipping the prince's remains to their homeland and, second, to continue in his footsteps.

Persad swiveled the massive chair, dialed the phone, and began speaking in an expressionless monotone. "The truck is out of service, my friend, but spare parts are on the way. The manufacturer has guaranteed replacement parts, so our truck should be operable very soon." Persad was anxious to get off the line. "Please rest assured, it will be repaired under full factory warranty. I will send confirmation later. Thank you."

His secretary signaled there was a call on hold. He lifted the still warm receiver and addressed the caller. "Mr. Seward, what a pleasant surprise. And how are things at Transcor, my friend? Have you good news?"

He listened attentively, then replied, "Yes, I will meet you there." He locked the desk and left instructions with the secretary that he would be in Washington for the rest of the day and into tomorrow. She was busily writing down his itinerary on a steno pad as he left.

Persad met Dan Seward at the east entrance to the White House, where they were met by two Secret Service officers, who accepted Seward's identification and Persad's consular name badge and ushered them through a single, nondescript door and down a flight of stairs. At the landing, they had their choice of two doors, each fitted with a television camera that was mounted flush into the ceiling. They chose the one on the left. The younger officer pushed slightly against the door, and its hydraulic motors slowly swung the door open into a room filled with desks and chairs, in no particular order. Strewn about were sport coats, parts of uniforms, caps, and other articles of clothing. Empty coffee mugs were everywhere.

They followed their hosts across the room as the elder officer greeted another who had slammed the door on the microwave and was reaching for the sugar. Quickly they were ushered into another room and down a corridor that led to a stairway leading one floor up. At the top, an officer inserted a plastic card into a slot next to the door, and the door opened automatically. It led to a narrow room with a single door at its end.

Seward had traveled the route before, conducting business, so he was no stranger to the Secret Service's routine. At the next door, the two officers motioned that Seward and Persad could enter, thanked them for their patience, and left.

The room was decorated in a distinguished colonial motif—beige and plum everywhere. Curtains, wallpaper, and even the furniture matched each other. Before they could sit in one of the antique chairs, a door on the opposite wall opened. It was the president's private secretary.

"Good day, gentlemen. Please follow me. The president is expecting you."

They entered one of the private offices of President Fenimore. It was pure business, no frills and no match for the offices of either Seward or the late prince. The president stood beside a conference table with a copy of the *Washington Post* in his hands. He placed it on the table and walked toward them as they entered. They shook hands and took their seats, Persad and Seward on one side of the big table and the president on the other. They got down to business.

The president started the conversation. "Gentlemen, thank you for coming. What can we do for you?"

Without hesitating, Seward began. "Thank you for seeing us, sir. You've heard, I'm sure, about the system being lost at sea."

"Yes, Dan. I have heard. Do we know what caused the crash at this point?" asked the president.

"No, Mr. President. We do not. It appears to be an act of God, or pilot error. I believe the FAA has ruled on it. But not withstanding their ruling, or its outcome, Prince Anini, excuse me, Mr. Persad must follow through. And, he'd be unable to do so unless you were to—"

"I know, Dan. I'm well aware of Transcor's position and yours, too." The president nodded to Persad. "And, please rest assured, gentlemen, we'll do all we can to accommodate your wishes." President Fenimore leaned back and stretched his arms skyward, then returned them to the bare tabletop, folding his hands. He addressed Persad.

"You, the prince, God rest his soul, and the king all know that your country honors the United States with your loyalty and—"

"Our oil?" interrupted Persad, in a monotone voice.

President Fenimore smiled and shook his head. "I can certainly appreciate your candor on that particular subject, but what I was going to say was how we appreciate your friendship. You are always welcome here, as are your staff and that of the king. We're all friends, and we deeply treasure that relationship."

"Sir, we have spoken with Ken Turner of Turner Engineering, and, outside of the timetable for raw materials and the like, there seems to be no problem in building another unit. It's the shipping method that causes us concern."

President Fenimore thought for a moment, leaned back again, and clasped his hands behind his neck. He pursed his lips and wrinkled his brow. "You know, until we are certain about the cause, certain measures will have to be taken."

"Do you have a way?" asked Seward.

President Fenimore relaxed his position and leaned forward in his chair, dropping his arms to the floor, where he shook out a few kinks. "It will need to be accomplished in complete secrecy, of course. On a need-to-know basis, you understand. Can your Transcor organization work with Turner Engineering to arrange a private enterprise deal? You understand what I'm saying?"

"Yes, sir. I think I do." Seward was glad to hear those words. "We can easily move the goods from Turner and onto another private aircraft as long as the eyes-only concept works at all ends."

"I follow you. Nothing will leave this office," assured President Fenimore. "And on that same subject, what precautions can be taken by Transcor and Turner to ensure that the, let's say, incident will not repeat itself?"

"I was just going to ask you the same thing, Mr. President," said Persad, his thick glasses perched high atop his nose.

"I've thought about that too and, quite frankly, am riding the fence on this one. I personally can guarantee that no government affiliates were involved in the crash. There would be no reason, except maybe the Pentagon was not that hot for the deal. From what I hear, it certainly wasn't a military operation, if you can even call it an operation."

It was well known in certain circles, including Seward's, that the president of the United States had little to say with regard to intelligence matters and, in fact at the time, did not sit on the intelligence board. From the CIA down to the lowest dealer in information commodities, no one ever sought the opinion of the White House, and they were probably justified, or so thought Daniel Seward.

"Mr. President, the guidance system is—"

"Dan, it isn't necessary for you to persuade me," the president interrupted "I fully understand the importance of this system to both the Saudis and our country, and the world, for that matter. With the good relations between our two countries growing with every passing day, its installation, as I like to refer to it, would secure the entire world, with us, the Americans and the Saudis, in complete control. Never again would the, shall we say, others pose a threat that we wouldn't be prepared to handle, if need be. So yes, Dan, I am in complete agreement with its vital importance. And, may I add, the country is thankful that you are brokering the deal, for we know that with you running things, they will be done. So, our hats are off to you." President Fenimore appeared pleased with himself.

"Can you ensure its safe delivery, Mr. President?" questioned Persad.

The president responded clearly, "Absolutely."

Daniel Seward knew that while President Fenimore's intentions were good, the man had no control of the situation and, therefore, depended entirely on his good associate,

Ken Turner, the manufacturer of the system. Would the shipment, indeed, arrive safely?

"Please excuse me, Mr. President, for being unfamiliar with the workings of the inner circle," Persad said. "But it appears to me, in my limited knowledge, that if you have a conflict with the Pentagon, wouldn't the CIA be naturally on your side? And, wouldn't it be, say, their responsibility or duty, as you will, to cover for you?

"Yes, that is true and probably is the case at this particular juncture. But, until the reports are in, I'm not taking any chances with this country's future, or that of yours. Does that make sense?"

"Absolutely, Mr. President." Persad changed positions in the soft chair, which squeaked under his weight. "Our country appreciates your concern, your loyalty, and your honesty."

"You're aware that the Pentagon is deeply concerned that along with our tracking and guiding system, which we've both agreed would protect the entire Arab region, go some very powerful trade secrets. Let's face it, gentlemen, we're giving away the whole boat based on some very strong basis points between your country and ours. Our defense would be open to you. In fact, ours would be identical except for a missing link that we would, of course, keep for ourselves."

Both Persad and Seward looked at each other in confusion. Seward was the first to question the president's last statement. "Missing link, Mr. President?"

"Come on now, Dan. You understand that for security purposes, whatever we deliver to Mr. Persad's country cannot jeopardize our country and, by the same token, their country cannot be jeopardized by ours. So, given the worst case scenario, not only would your country be safe from intrusion by anyone, including the United States, we, in turn, would be safe from intrusion by the same forces. Gentlemen, that's good politics." He smiled proudly.

Seward made a quick decision that as long as the president and Ken Turner were on friendly terms, and as long as Turner knew that the president had authorized him to build another system, all would be fine. The system would be built. That was all he hoped for in today's meeting.

President Fenimore stood and extended his hand to each, and without a word, the door through which Persad and Seward had entered, opened, and a Secret Service officer bid them exit.

As the two men walked toward the door, Seward lagging behind Persad a few steps, the president spoke softly but firmly. "Dan," he said. "A word please."

Seward motioned to Persad, who nodded his understanding that he would wait in the corridor until the president was finished with Seward.

Seward closed the door behind him and walked closer to the president. "Yes sir?"

"Dan," the president began in a near whisper. "You're aware of the situation here, correct?"

"Yes, sir. I'm aware of it," Seward replied, although not really sure he meant it.

"Election time is not far away," the president continued. "I'm afraid there are some who think it's time for my retirement, if you follow me."

"I think I do, Mr. President." Thoughts of the CIA, Pentagon, State Department, FBI, and others flashed through his mind in a split second as he answered.

"Good. Then you would probably not be all that surprised to learn that the intelligence community is not entirely behind me on this one."

"I understand, sir," Seward replied, but again was not entirely sure of his answer. "And, the significance is?"

"The significance is simple," President Fenimore explained. "Tactically, this country needs the stability in the Arab world, which can only be accomplished through our ties with the Saudis. You see, Dan, this system is the key factor in ensuring that tie and, I might add, ensuring our stability."

"You mean the Arab world's?" Seward asked

"Yes, Dan. You see, their stability is our stability. We depend on each other."

"For oil," Seward interjected.

"Oh yes," the president concurred, showing a brief sign of redness on his face. "But more than that, Middle East peace is a thing of the future, and I aim to see it happen within the next four years, no matter what. Can you understand that, Dan?"

Seward understood perfectly what Fenimore was up to—reelection. "Well, not exactly, sir.

"You must trust me on this, Dan. I'm counting on you to work with Ken Turner to build a new system and see that it is safely deposited into the hands of our friends, the Saudis. Bortens may be the best bet, but I'll leave that up to you as long as you use a private carrier and, I don't have to remind you, as discretely as possible.

"I understand completely, Mr. President." There was little question in Seward's mind about why the president was so secretive about this project. The CIA was against it. Hell, he was not sure that the Pentagon was behind it either. Oh well, as long as his company, Transcor, and Ken Turner's made out on the deal, all would be well.

At that moment, the door reopened, revealing the Secret Service agent. Seward knew the conversation was now over, so he nodded his agreement with the president and rejoined Persad.

ELEVEN

Dean Cavalli began each day when the sun rose, and planned every minute of every hour until sunset. Then he would stuff his papers into a tidy briefcase and head for home in the back seat of a limo, memorizing what he needed to accomplish the following day. At the drop of a hat, he could recite his schedule minute by minute and subject by subject. He left his office precisely at nine thirty each night and was back at six thirty the next morning. But as neat and tidy as was his pace, he had a weakness.

He was a desk man lacking street smarts, a strange resume for the director of the CIA, having been the chief of several overseas bureaus and an expert in foreign operations. He was a manipulator who chose to buy his information, insulating himself from the dirt and depending instead on the talents of others in his employ.

He was a well-dressed man—starched, button-down shirt with a diagonally striped tie and spit-shined wingtips.

He had the president's ear, which he guarded to the degree that it fit his and the country's best interests. He was spirited and full of energy and had a near-perfect photographic memory. Cavalli was only forty-five, but he had the experience of a sixty-year-old and the physique of a college quarterback. This was his third morning appointment, and he had many to go before lunch.

"What can we do to stir things up this morning, Dean?" the president asked.

He pulled back one of the chairs of the conference table. "Do you mind?"

"Please," replied the president who then sat opposite.

"We've been discussing our position throughout the world, especially in the Middle East. I have met with the bureau chiefs, and generally the consensus is this: We need to protect ourselves, and for a couple of reasons. I don't have to go into them, except to say we need their oil as much as they need our protection. Agreed?"

The president gnawed on a pencil eraser, then tapped it on the bare table a couple of times, and then laid it still, folding his hands. He liked to be right. "Yes, except for another thing. As much as we protect ourselves and our allies over there, I'm still bothered by aggressions from other countries, including those in Asia."

"Sir, I couldn't agree with you more," Cavalli said. "But, for the sake of argument, let's stick to the Middle East. When we last talked about sending them a satellite guidance system similar to ours, with a few modifications of course, it concerned me, and now it concerns others in the community. Let me explain."

"Please do, Dean."

"I know you feel that arming Saudi Arabia is the key to peace in their surrounding nations. I must not confuse Middle East security with politics—"

"Hold it, Dean," president Fenimore interrupted. "You're referring to my reelection campaign?"

"Well, sir, and please excuse me if I'm not in tune to your politics. Frankly, I could care less unless, of course, it affects our security. May I continue?"

"Please." The president was careful not to show his pending anger.

"I wish to make certain that whatever decision is made is not made too hastily. Having said that, let me explain. The fact that you're up for reelection, and I'm certainly on your side, Mr. President, may backfire if the wrong decision is made and the press, in their infinite wisdom, ever get their hands on it. Hell, Mr. President, they'd have a heyday with it, and you'd be literally burned at the stake. So, that's where I'm coming from."

"I see, Dean," replied the president, knowing full well that Cavalli was not in his camp. "And thank you for your support. I do understand and hope you know that whatever you decide will occur, I'll see to it." The president's tongue was deeply embedded in his cheek.

"Thank you for understanding, Mr. President. I know you feel the nation's sympathies are out to the Saudis because of the always-present danger posed by the Iraqis and, for that matter, the Iranians and Syrians. And don't forget the Turks. Although we have our aircraft planted on their soil, they're putting up with us until someone else makes them a better deal. At any rate, we all agree that our relationship with the Saudis is an important one and that we should protect that until our dying days."

"Or until the oil well runs dry?"

"Well, no question about it. It's an important factor."

"Well, at least we agree on one thing, Dean. You know, of course, that I have authorized Ken Turner of Turner Engineering to build another system and that Dan Seward's Transcor organization still remains the broker in the deal?" The president enjoyed besting the other man. "You're aware of that, aren't you?"

Cavalli sat rigid, knowing no matter what he thought, the president would do exactly as he pleased, as long as it suited his reelection purposes. He humored him. "I understand that, sir, but only wish you had consulted with me first."

"Hell, Dean, we talked about this months ago. You pretty much agreed it was necessary."

Cavalli remembered agreeing with him more or less to shut him up until he could find another solution. In the back of his mind, although he hoped the president's idea would simply go away, he knew it wouldn't and should have known, too, the system was well on the way. He also knew his future was dependent, in part, on some of his own politicking.

He regarded President Fenimore as a control freak, which he disagreed with but, nonetheless, gave him credit for, realizing it might be a necessary element for a man in charge of the largest and most powerful nation in the world. Offhand, he seemed right for the job. But he was a phony.

Eleven

He worked on his image like a sculptor. He would throw out names of people whom he felt gave him stature. What was more, it seemed to work, for the present at least. The man seemed exclusively concerned with appearances and reelection. Reality was something to be buried well out of sight. Cavalli knew it was useless to argue with the chief, since he'd already made up his mind.

"And so, Mr. President, I will speak to the others."

The two men stood, and Cavalli left the room. Before the door closed behind him, President Fenimore echoed, "Thanks, Dean, for your support. If I can assist in any other way, don't hesitate—"

The door closed before the president finished. Cavalli knew his place so well that if he valued his job as head of the CIA, and he certainly did, a little more politicking would be in order. But once again, it would be Cavalli's own brand. He pressed a number on his cell phone and waited.

The other end answered, "Amacon."

"I'm afraid we've played all our cards, and not one single ace," Cavalli spoke softly. "You know what to do."

TWELVE

It was a typical fall day in the nation's capital, although the remains of summer lingered well into October, making the weather slightly warm, with just a hint of humidity To Bill Gale, it was the prettiest time of year. The slightly heavy air rose from the Potomac, moving across the balcony and through the open sliding door. It brought with it the first stream of morning light.

He rose to meet the morning sun. It was barely a day since he'd left Dominique safely in New York City. Now, he was back in familiar territory. He'd spent years in and around the Washington area, and was now close enough to his old stomping grounds in Langley that he could roust the gate guards with a well-tossed stone. He checked the clock on the nightstand and stripped for a hot shower. The water pressure was strong, and the heat felt especially comforting as he envisioned the day's events, hoping they'd go as planned. He'd been around the spying business for over twenty years, and since the government's security policies made him sick, he was only too happy to be on his own. As an agent, he'd never allowed himself to act on his hunches without being keenly aware of where he was headed. As he grew in corporate espionage circles, he learned to move only when he felt comfortable. It didn't necessarily mean he had to have solid evidence, either. He had certain feelings about his old instructor, the senator, and most were positive. Some, however, were shaky, and that's what upset him most. He had to be careful not to let his emotional ties taint his judgment.

A quick glass of water and he was out the door. He slid his room key across the marble counter to the desk clerk, who was in the midst of paperwork for an elderly couple checking in. He took advantage of the hotel's instant check out, grabbed a *Washington Post* from the lobby dispenser, and gave his room number to the bellman, who took off in a hurry to fetch his rental car.

The short drive south along Military Road was, in the old days, a scenic one. But now, it seemed like everyone was in on it, with retail shops and restaurants popping up everywhere. A real urban sprawl. His destination, as described by Senator Brewer, was a five-story office building situated between two strip centers. He spotted it, a product of the mid-eighties, he supposed, with ample parking between freshly bark-dusted islands of trees and ivy.

Off the lobby was a convenience store where, inside, a lit candle exhaled its aromatic scent into the lobby, giving a pleasant and peaceful old-time country atmosphere to the lobby's stark and officious presentation. Other than a newspaper stand, though, the lobby itself was void of furniture and fixtures. A large mural opposite the two elevators interrupted the black and white marbled walls. It depicted the Gettysburg battlefield.

Gale entered the first available elevator, in which two men were standing already, looking nonchalant, newspapers folded under their arms; both dressed in ho-hum business suits. Since a basement level wasn't identified in the row of buttons, he suspected that either the two men had missed their floor as the elevator came down or they were professional elevator riders, otherwise known as the building's security force. The senator's instructions were to take the car to the fifth floor. Gale punched the corresponding button, but the car came to a quick stop at the second floor. The doors opened, revealing two uniformed men. One had a shotgun aimed at the floor, while the other asked for Gale's identification but not those of the other two men, confirming his suspicions. The unarmed guard stepped into the elevator car, inserted a key into a slot, pressed a green button at the top of the console, and stepped out as the doors closed. Upon reaching his floor, Gale got out, while the other two riders remained.

Although the fifth floor appeared to be a typical business office, Gale was sure it wasn't. He'd come to expect nearly anything in the intelligence community, especially when information from nearly every imaginable source passed through the communication lines of this office, or so he imagined, as well as those in other offices in the greater Washington vicinity. Nothing was ever thrown away but rather was stored in volumes of tapes, disks, and other files to rest until anyone with any clearance wished to discover that his dad attended a meeting of the International Workers of the World on August 3, 1943. And for that, his dad could've been labeled a Communist. It was when the serious and the nonsensical data, like his dad's reference as a commie, collided that he became concerned.

A counter ran from side to side, directly in front of the elevator doors. He followed the senator's instructions beyond the counter to the first private office. As he approached, his old friend the senator opened the door and bid him welcome.

"It's nice to see you, senator. You're looking better."

The senator motioned for Gale to take the only seat that was opposite a small metal desk piled high with files. "Better than what?" he asked, as he stuffed his husky frame into the swivel chair. He was a typical, aging, athletic type who had gotten too busy to care about his physical condition. A little paunchy, his fair skin and brownish gray, bushy hair still gave him the necessary looks to get by in the Capitol city. His mustache matched his hair coloring. He was aristocratic and businesslike and yet likeable. He was friendly and not necessarily for a purpose.

"Have you been out to sea lately?" Gale asked. "Are you still a sailor?"

"Nope," replied Senator Brewer. "That's for the younger kids. Mine's got a motor. Thirty-six-footer, twin screws, all the gadgets."

"Still keep it at the same place?" Gale asked, as he renewed their friendship.

"Same place, Chesapeake. Pretty close to here and always a full liquor cabinet, I might add. Since I gave up smoking, boozing is about my only sin."

Twelve

"It'll kill you nearly as fast," Gale joked. "What about the family?"

"Both girls in college in Boston and that's it. One's on a full ride and the other? Well, let's just say she doesn't take after her mother."

"Speaking of which—"

"You know what, she's still at the old firm. Haven't seen her in a while." He changed the subject. "You'd think that two lawyers in the family would be enough. Julie's going to be one too. That is, if I don't run out of money."

Gale had heard that they'd split the sheets a few years back and wondered if they were still apart. He remembered that both the senator and his wife had been practicing attorneys in the same law firm for a few years before the senator joined the CIA some thirty years ago. Gale thought about asking why his old friend left the intelligence business, but decided to cut to the chase.

"So, senator, I need your help."

"Sounds like it," replied the Senator. "You're getting into something, you know that."

"Can you tell me what?"

Senator Brewer stopped for a moment and continued. "I can only tell you that government contracts are a guarded commodity and people will do anything to protect their interests in them."

"So what's your interest in all this?" asked Gale.

"I'm on the intelligence board, as you probably know. For obvious reasons."

"I seem to remember that you spent some time in the Soviet Union," Gale added.

"Not long," the senator replied. "But too long. If you had stuck around, you'd probably have been there too. Or in East Germany somewhere running a damn warehouse for some phony Kraut organization."

"I got bounced."

"Like hell, you did," the senator replied. "You were good, but you just had this hang-up."

"About not having my nuts on the chopping block?"

"About fearing deep cover. We would've taken care of you."

"That's a crock. You know damn well that if I disappeared, none of my family would have known where I was, and neither the CIA nor the Defense Department would've told them. 'We're sorry, but we have no one working for us by that name.' You know that anyway."

"I do. Sorry I brought it up."

"Ah, Senator, there is one thing I'd like to ask of you."

"Anything, as long as it's not too illegal," the senator quipped.

"I need a couple of IDs. Ones that will gain me access to anywhere I need to go in Washington," said Gale.

"How far up?" asked Senator Brewer.

"I guess there's no way to reach the president, but getting into the White House would help. Along with the IDs, I need a background as well," Gale said.

"National Security Agency works very well, as will a paid mercenary," suggested the senator.

"NSA will open all the respectable doors, but why the mercenary angle?" Gale asked.

"Like the good old days, remember?" replied the senator. "NSA will open all the respectable doors."

"Got it," said Gale. "So, what about the other one?"

"The not-so-respectable ones," the senator answered as he raised a single eyebrow, and slowly nodded his head, while winking. "I'll make the phone calls to set up the background, in case someone should check up on you. The IDs will be delivered to you in the morning.

"Thank you senator," Gale signed. "I knew I could count on you."

Anyway, let's get back to the task at hand." Senator Brewer checked his watch. "I've got a meeting in a few minutes, but this might help."

He slid a file folder across the desk. On the tab was printed the name "TRANSCOR." Inside, it contained a single sheet of paper with three lines of type showing the name and address of Transcor's Frankfurt office. That was it. Transcor must be important he mused. The mere fact that the senator had their data confirmed their importance within the community.

"I see." Gale studied the sheet of paper and eyed the senator. His response confirmed the room was probably bugged. "Is there something—"

"Tonight, stay in the Roosevelt Hotel," the Senator ordered.

Since he'd been cut off in mid-sentence for obvious reasons, he figured the senator picked up on it. He stood and extended his hand to his old friend. "Thank you, sir."

It was a short drive to Falls Church and the Roosevelt Hotel. Since the senator recommended it, he assumed it was unlike every other hotel in the greater Washington area and not owned by the CIA. He checked in, using a fictitious name that would be recognizable to the senator, told the clerk where he'd be, in case of any messages, and went directly to the bar, where he ordered a dry martini and took advantage of their free hors d'oeuvres. At about ten, he retired to a small but beautifully restored room filled with antique furniture.

He plopped himself onto the bed, fully clothed, and pressed the remote until it rested on the first sports channel. He hadn't realized he had dozed off, when a noise startled him. He rose quickly to see a manila envelope lying on the carpet in front of the door, one corner resting under the closed door. Inside, he found three perfect ID cards encased in plastic.

The photos of him was a few years old, but one matched the date that the State Department fictitiously hired a Richard Larson. Another identified him with the same name, working for the NSA. A third named him O'Malley, mercenary for hire, with a phone number for anyone who doubted his existence to call.

The State Department ID would provide credibility for his portrayal of a import specialist for goods entering the United States, exported from Europe. He said his silent thanks to the senator and replaced his other ID with the new one. To complete his cover and set the plan into motion, the next morning he called the State Department and asked for Mr. Larson to verify that he was, indeed, a trusted employee. If anyone should dare question his authority, they could always call his office in Washington for verification. He didn't bother phoning NSA nor the number on the mercenary ID. He silently thanked the senator.

THIRTEEN

The weather was clear, and the Atlantic looked peaceful from thirty-two thousand feet. Bill Gale remembered an assignment at Thule Air Force Base, on the western shore of Greenland, where the air force kept watch on the rest of the world, especially the Soviet Union. A critical part of the Ballistic Missile Early Warning System or DEW line, he had been impressed that the radar picked up a MIG jet sitting idle on a Moscow airfield. He turned his thoughts to the task at hand.

Assuming his new cover as a State Department inspector, Gale had plenty of reasons to visit Germany and, in this particular instance, Frankfurt. The fluctuating exchange rate had been an ever-looming problem to American buyers, who fought hard to keep their prices in line with those of their competitors. A good enough reason for this visit was to ensure that the German manufacturers he chose to visit were responsible enough to keep their product lines up to snuff. Under this inspector's watchful eye, there would be no shortchanging the American buyers with inferior components.

He got into deep cover by creating his job and a short history from which to base his experiences. He fabricated prior assignments, giving each one a job description, a name, and an untraceable location. His new assignment would include the inspection of cargoes, businesses, warehouses, docks, and anything else he fictitiously chose to get him inside to get some answers. Beginning with the last contrived assignment, he went through each one from start to finish, reliving each one as though it had really happened.

Mentally, he took himself back to a Washington office, filled with three or four file cabinets and a neatly organized desk that matched his working habits. A couple of chairs were set against a stark white wall bearing scuff marks from the chairs having been pushed against it. A framed photo of the Washington Monument and Reflecting Pond on one wall, a window with mini-blinds on another, a golf trophy resting squarely atop one of the file cabinets along with some customs manuals between a set of bookends on yet another and, finally, the door and window completed the last one. Typical government maintenance of the pair of overhead fluorescent fixtures, mounted flush against the acoustic ceiling tile, ensured that one would certainly flicker. And so it did, making his office real in a way that, should the need arise, his description of normal day-to-day affairs would certainly be convincing. No slipups and no second chances.

Thirteen

He slipped deeper and deeper into cover until he was, in all reality, Richard Larson of the State Department. He took the fake ID from his wallet and studied the photo of a younger Bill Gale, while rehearsing a short sentence or two to explain how his department never quite got around to updating his photo ID. Mentally, he discarded his real name and now became Richard Larson.

On schedule, the 747's wheels touched down with a thump at the Frankfurt International Airport. Despite the fact that he had spent many weeks on both sides of the Berlin Wall back in the early seventies, he could not help feeling a shiver of excitement at being back in Germany. From the air, the countryside had looked like a peaceful collection of forests and farmlands. Shades of green were everywhere, a stark difference to where he was headed, deep inside Frankfurt's industrial district. Crossing the impossibly crowded streets, they reminded him of Manhattan, except Frankfurt's were much cleaner.

Formalities at the airport were swift. As he waited to claim his bag, an airport security team composed of an officer and a German shepherd meandered through the crowd. As the carousel began turning, the team got to work, sniffing for contraband.

Richard Larson's reservations at Hotel Montinore were in order. The sun had set and the nightlife was well underway. It could just as well have been the middle of the day. All the streetlights were on, and most doorways were ablaze with colored lights. The crowd slowly meandering through the square, while some stood huddled together, speaking and gesturing to each other, reminded him of Oktoberfest. Across the square, the windows in the office high-rises were all ablaze. But, he had no interest in celebrating. Right now he needed his rest.

After a good night's sleep, he sipped coffee from a room service cart, patted his wallet to be sure he had everything, and gathered his things. Even at such an early hour, the lobby was busy with international travelers checking in and out. Luggage was piled in a heap near a counter where the bellman struggled to keep some kind of order. Gale walked to the counter and received simple directions to the general area of Transcor's office building. He was careful not to draw any attention to either the name of Transcor or the fact that an American State Department official had asked for directions to it.

Around one corner took him before a mass of apartment buildings, five to ten stories high. They were jammed together as though they'd been subject to Harlem's building codes. The difference, though, was apparent. These buildings were clean as a pin—no wires stretched between them, and no clothes hung out to dry. He also noticed the absence of old junker cars leaning against the curbs.

Another turn took him into the commercial downtown area with office buildings and shops. Although it resembled many American cities, again the neatness reminded him of some years past when he'd spent some time in and out of East Germany, where the towns on both sides of the wall were spotlessly clean. Gale spotted Transcor's building in the next block.

He grasped the brass handle and pulled the massive glass door toward him. The decor spelled money—marbled floors throughout the spacious foyer. Small evergreens in brick planters formed a forested boundary from the foyer to the hallway that led to what he expected were the more elite of Frankfurt's executive offices. A single, oval table stood in the middle of the foyer. It was made of black marble, and it served as the receptionist's desk. She was petite, with short red hair and a smattering of freckles on her rosy cheeks. He guessed her age to be around thirty.

"Good Morning, Do you speak English?" he asked.

She smiled, and her rosy cheeks became rosier. "Oh yes. I was raised there. Are you an American?" she replied. Her accent was only slight.

"Yes. Oh excuse me." What luck, he thought, as he presented his fake ID.

She took the plastic ID and slightly skimmed it, then returned it with another smile. "State Department? Welcome to Frankfurt," she said. "By the way, my name is Carolyn."

He was in! Now, if he could just continue his charm and win her over, he'd have everything he wanted.

"Nice to meet you, Carolyn. I'm Richard Larson, State Department." He continued. "But you know that already. Actually, I'm a commodities expert. The reason I'm here is to look at your export log. Do you have the authority to show me around?" He was well practiced at developing instant personality shifts to suit his purpose at any moment. And, depending on his target's responsiveness, he'd either win their undaunted support or get lost in the attempt, at which point a hasty retreat might not leave him any more options for returning.

"Oh yes, Mr. Larson. I would be pleased to show you around." She stood and placed her headset on the desktop and hit the intercom button. "Alisa, Carolyn. Can you help us please?"

Alisa promptly arrived at the reception area, while Carolyn stepped around the desk. She held out her hand, and led Inspector Larson past several of Transcor's private offices, describing the occupant of each one, including titles and general duties. Although he figured she was pretty much his at this point, he was still careful not to waver from the typically governmental posture that he'd introduced minutes before. He wasn't yet sure of her capabilities and wondered what her level of knowledge was about Transcor.

"Describe what you do here, Carolyn. I mean, I take it you're more than a receptionist."

"Oh yes, forgive me. I'm the programmer—computer, you know. In the States, I worked for all sorts of software companies and became somewhat proficient in American customs' requirements, duty fees, plus direct links to the brokers and the like."

"How did you get over here?" he asked.

"I've been here for about ten years," she replied. "Not at Transcor, because I've been here only five years. I was with several companies doing contract work. Basically I was self-employed. I installed software and brought my clients online. In fact, that's how I began here. Eventually, though, they liked what they saw and offered me a pretty nifty position. It's pretty soft and, well, I sort of have the run of the place."

Bingo, Gale thought. She was perfect and exactly what he needed. He stepped in front of her, interrupting their journey down the hallway. "Wait a second. I have an idea," he said as he stood there, arms crossed. "The State Department is interested in Transcor's exports to the United States. How tough is it to retrieve, say, this fiscal year's data?"

She touched his wrist with both hands and said, "Follow me."

Carolyn led him into a large room lined with file cabinets and a pair of computers. She pulled a swivel chair over to one computer, sat down, and began hitting various keys. The screen came alive with data as she moved the mouse around the pad, clicking here and there. It came to rest on a heading that read "Exports—United States." "I'll print it out. It's about twenty pages, so it'll take a minute or two." She turned to face him. "Are you sure you won't take a cup of coffee, Mr. Larson?"

"Oh, no thank you, Carolyn. And please, as long as we're alone, there's no need to be so formal. Call me Richard." He sat on the corner of the desk. "By the way, is there a place we can go that's private, where we can analyze this?

"Of course, follow me." She led him down the hall to the front desk where she told Alisa, in perfect German, that she'd be out for the rest of the day. She took him to a pub a couple of blocks away.

If the place had been in his hometown, the Health Department would have had a fit, with inches of sawdust covering the floor. Railings between booths appeared to be hand sculpted from small branches that Gale visualized as having been gathered from somewhere deep within Germany's Black Forest. The booths' back rests were also hand carved with little faces of elves who used to guard the same forest but now were simply peering at those who dare to sit with their backs to them. Cuckoo clocks of every description adorn the walls high enough for their winding chains to hang unobstructed to the floor.

The staff wore colorful period costumes as they served the midday meal. Sawdust sopped up the splashes of spilled beer as a musician clad in lederhosen played German folk songs on his accordion. Larson and Carolyn were shown to a booth about halfway back.

"Want a Bud Light?" she asked playfully, elbows on the table.

"Sure, like I could get it." He pushed his back against the solid wood bench.

A young man, his lederhosen, damp from a recent spill, set a tall mug in the middle of the table and walked away. Their menu was printed on the sides of the empty mug, offering the usual specialty dishes. Larson's only hunger was for information, so he passed on food for now, assuming Carolyn felt the same way. He slid the mug to the side.

The waiter returned and Carolyn ordered for them. "Two lagers please."

To Larson, Carolyn was a commodity. A lady who was in charge of recording millions of dollars worth of exports and other business activities of Transcor's vast enterprises. He figured she knew the precise location of every Transcor shipment, when it left, and when it arrived. But, he needed more than that. He needed data on the people who ran Transcor. He studied her expressions, as she nervously looked for the waiter, hoping her bit of anxiety was more as a result of her possibly being interested in him. The beer came, and the foam spilled over the frosty mug and down onto the planked table.

"Cheers," she said, clinking the heavy mug against his.

He returned her toast and followed her lead. But his mind was far from the beer. Anxious to move forward, he checked his watch and yet was careful not to alter the speed with which he continued. He didn't wish to trigger any unforeseen responses. "By the way, how much pull do you have?"

Just as he hoped, she took the question simply and replied as such. "Quite a bit. What did you have in mind?" she asked.

He chose his words carefully. "Oh, for instance, we need to update our files with new stockholders, new officers, and basically any other changes, ownership or otherwise, that may have occurred in the past few years."

"I can get you that." She took another sip, lowered the mug to the table, and grabbed a few peanuts, which she began shelling one by one, discarding the empty shells onto the sawdust floor. "Anything in particular?"

He was absolutely amazed at how easily it was going so far. "Let's begin with current ownership, top-ranking officers, executives, their bios, anything else that would give me a clear picture of who's running things." A planned pause. "Oh yes, and anything about your key executive's associations and memberships on boards or political action committees, any associations with American military and others." He flashed a big smile as he went for the most damaging data he could. "You might also throw in anything associated with our American politicians and, if you have it, anything on recent travels abroad, especially Egypt, Saudi Arabia, Turkey, and other places around there. You know, the works, anything that would show ties to us or other governments."

Gracefully, she popped a shelled peanut into her mouth, threw the shell to the floor, and chewed the peanut for a while, followed by a sip of beer. "OK, I can get you that." Then she looked into Richard Larson's undercover eyes, moistened her lips, and asked, "Anything else?"

He had to admit that it was tempting, but he stuck to business. He needed the information worse than he needed a one-night stand. He actually had a tough time believing his good fortune. He speculated what would happen if he asked her to bring the data to his hotel room. He decided to ask anyway and let the chips fall where they may.

"I don't suppose it's possible, but can you get the information today and meet me at my hotel later? I mean, you've checked out for the day and all—"

"No problem, Richard," she interrupted. She finished her beer and eased forward on the bench, elbows on the table, hands cupping her chin. "Where are you staying?"

"I'm at the Montinore."

She grabbed her purse and gracefully slid out of the booth and stood on the sawdust floor, peanut shells cracking under her shoes. She winked and said, "Give me a couple of hours?"

Thirteen

"You got it. See you in a while." He remained seated as she left. Her walk was hurried but poised as she left the pub.

He was amused at the thought of Carolyn being so anxious to please him. Was it that she was taken in by his being an American? He had no idea and couldn't care less. At this point, information was his main concern.

So far, Gale was pleased with his cover identity as he continued to think of himself as Richard Larson, and only Richard Larson. Back at the Montinore, he gathered his personal items, went to the lobby, and checked out. The bar was off the lobby. He picked a stool that was at a vantage point from which he could spot Carolyn as she entered the hotel's lobby. He ordered a martini and waited.

Barely an hour had passed when he spotted her at the front desk. He guessed she'd just received the news that he had checked out and had turned to walk away when he caught her attention. She seemed relieved at seeing him. She nearly ran to the small cocktail table, grasping both of his hands with hers as her handbag's shoulder straps dropped from her shoulder to rest on her forearms.

"Care for a drink?" he offered.

At first she hesitated but then acquiesced. "OK. But I thought—"

"I know, I know," said Larson. "I've been called away suddenly…to Munich."

Although he had only just met her, he felt a little guilty about leading her on. It was the one thing for which he had not been prepared. Then he had a thought. What if she walks away, data and all?

His fears were forgotten as she took a file folder from her bag and laid it on the table. "It's all there," Carolyn said. "Everything including how the company was founded, customer and vendor lists, CEO file. It's all there." With elbows on the table, she cradled her chin in her open hands. "Am I ever going to see you again?"

True, at this point he had what he came for. "Carolyn, I'm terribly sorry; I have to go," Larson explained. "What say, though, we make a promise to each other to get together in the near future? I'll be back soon, and, if you give me your address and phone number, I'll stay in touch, and we can plan something. Never can tell when you might need a job back home, and I know a lot of people."

She gave him a little girl sigh. "I can go along with that. Do you have time for another drink?"

"Let me see." He checked his watch and thought for a moment. "I really don't. I should get to the airport. Do you want to ride out there with me?" He knew what her answer would be.

"I'd really like to, but I have a few things to do." She stood and extended her hand.

But Larson wouldn't settle for a handshake. "I think I'd settle for a hug." He spoke no words as he embraced her. She pressed her lips against his neck, and he kissed her cheek. She pulled away from him and with a wink, turned and left the bar. Both knew they'd not see each other again.

Once inside the plane, Gale emerged from his Richard Larson cover and patted his briefcase containing the newly acquired information on Transcor. He lowered the tray table and released his seat belt, then turned on the overhead light. He laid the file folder on the flat surface and thumbed through the papers. One page contained a brief description on Daniel Seward, naming him as the founder and chief executive officer. The next one was a complete surprise— James Fenimore? That was it. No further description; just the name of the president of the United States.

Another page's content was supposed to be a list of vendors, but it listed only one—Turner Engineering. The customer file page, too, listed a single customer—Abdul Anini. Missing, though, was anything to tie it all together. The president? He wondered about that.

He spent the rest of the trip in silent rumination, having mixed feelings about the number he had run on Carolyn, giving it far too much importance. But he couldn't help it. Probably the one single flaw that kept him from excelling in the government spy business was the single asset that kept him sane. He had a conscience.

Gale was glad to be on familiar turf, even if it was a hotel in the Big Apple. The night clerk threw his room key on the countertop, where it slid into Gale's open hand. A short elevator ride and a brisk walk down the hall to their room, and, within seconds, he'd be there with Dominique.

FOURTEEN

Dominique had Gale up and showered at the crack of dawn for a big Western breakfast of ham and eggs, hash browns, and fresh, buttered toast served with piping hot coffee from the room service cart. As they ate, the warm sun peeked through the open blinds onto the plush carpet. She was lovely. Her wet hair was combed straight down, covering the collar of the hotel terry cloth robe. Her feet were bare and still wet from the shower, and the shampoo's fragrance filled the air. He wanted to linger awhile longer, but the Bortens time clock was ticking away, compelling him to get back to it.

He pushed himself away from the small table and went to her and took her into his arms "I want you to stay here and keep the door locked, just as before, OK?" He gave her one last squeeze then headed out the door.

The valet left the driver's door open. Gale got in, and drove away from the curb, heading for the nearest parking space. Barely a block away, he pulled over and turned off the rental car's engine. From the briefcase, he retrieved his notes from the day before. In a separate compartment, he sifted through an array of plastic ID cards, searching until he found it. There it was. Richard Larson—IRS Internal Auditor—Ogden, Utah. It was the same name, but it would still work perfectly. It would be easy to become Richard Larson again.

* * * * * * * * * *

West Thames is a short street that dead-ended at Battery Place in the southernmost section of Manhattan. On the south side of Thames Street, hidden from view from the main entrance to Turner Engineering's New York office, stood a most skilled mechanic. A long list of prior assignments had fetched Jopaq very profitable notoriety. This one would be no different. Sure, he'd miscalculated a time or two. But it was all in the odds of the game. A game that he was confident in winning. In his world, the concept of win-win didn't exist. Only win-lose. The devious, deadly, and highly skilled mechanic was ready. He continued his watch, waiting for the right moment.

* * * * * * * * * *

From the Transcor files, Richard Larson had learned that, although Turner maintained their executive offices in New York City, their main manufacturing and engineering facility was in Washington, D.C. He had a feeling there was more to discover within their accounting department, so this was his target. He entered the office reception area. A young lady sat at the receptionist's desk inside the glass double doors. She looked up as he approached her.

"Good morning. I'm with the Internal Revenue Service." He flashed his ID and held it there for a few moments until her eyes shifted to his. When they did, he continued to play out his script.

"Name's Larson. I'd like to see whoever is in charge of your inventories."

Past experiences told him not to ask for a specific person but to generalize and let the target do the recommending. The chance of her recalling an IRS inspector asking to see a Mr. So-and-So was statistically much higher. He knew he'd wind up with their controller or chief operating officer anyway. It was a simple, but nonetheless effective, smoke screen.

"That would be our controller or perhaps purchasing." She seemed eager to satisfy.

Richard Larson always chose the guy on the top rung. His experience had proven that those in the middle of the ladder most often had an agenda that may compromise his own. Corporate climbers are a dangerous impediment to any mission simply because of their concern for being right at the expense of making others appear wrong.

"Your controller please," Richard Larson replied. "And that would be Mr. ah—"

"Mr. Kelly. Mr. James Kelly. I'll ring him for you." She pushed a button on the phone console and asked Richard Larson to wait.

Within a few minutes, a fiftyish man in a three-piece suit walked past the reception toward Larson, who was alone in the lobby. "Mr. Larson, I'm Jim Kelly. Please." He motioned for him to follow him to the first office on the left. Upon reaching the door to his office, Kelly stopped and leaned against the door jamb with his outstretched arm leaning against the opposite jamb, as though to block Gale's entrance. "What can I do for you, Mr. Larson?"

Richard Larson replied, "I faxed a memo earlier this morning to your attention. But if your secretary hasn't brought it to you, then perhaps I can fill you in briefly."

"That would be fine, sir."

"We're concerned about inventories, in particular. Your corporate return has been accepted, as filed, for the prior fiscal year and would have been for this year…" Richard Larsen paused for effect.

"But what?" Kelly inquired. He was beginning to show some concern, but not to the point of divulging anything he shouldn't.

"It seems that your inventory conversion formula is inconsistent with prior years," Richard Larson explained. "Are you responsible for that particular calculation, or do you have others who compute your final inventories?" It was his guess that Kelly would be familiar with the formula since it had a direct impact on their gross profit calculations. Richard Larson was counting on the fact that a company this size would certainly have an assistant to handle the formula, leaving its final review up to Kelly.

"We've been using the same formula for the past eight years, and, if my memory serves me correctly, it was because of a prior audit that we did. So, we're still doing the formula as your people suggested. No changes, unless of course—"

"You were flagged," Richard Larson interrupted. "And, that's the reason for my visit today. I'm sure it must have been a mistake, but once I review your formula and look at its audit trail, if you've maintained consistency, my report will reflect as much."

"I understand, Mr. Larson."

Richard Larson continued, "As for time and inconvenience to Turner Engineering, assuming you grant IRS access to both your computer and whoever performed the inputs, we're talking an hour or so."

As of yet, there was no sign that Kelly was going to cooperate and allow Richard Larson the run of the computer. Kelly was firm, half in and half out his office doorway. "You wish to access our system? Well that's—"

"If, on the other hand, your people are unavailable and it becomes necessary to corner you, personally, for the data, we would be looking at a few days, minimum. That would be your choice, Mr. Kelly."

"Well sir, I believe I can accommodate you." Kelly released his grip on the doorjamb and motioned Richard Larson inside, where he picked up the phone. "Rachel, please clear a desk and make sure the computer is functioning. I'm sending Mr. Larson, from the IRS, down to see you. Please cooperate with him and give him a brief overview of our operating system so that he may have full access to our inventory program and journal entries. He'll be there in a few moments."

He cradled the receiver and scribbled her name and office number on a post-it and handed it to Richard Larson. "She is expecting you. Stay as long as you like and make yourself comfortable. Can I—"

"Thank you, Mr. Kelly," he interrupted, realizing he had pulled it off.

Kelly led him down a hallway to an office with most of the floor space taken up by desks and tables on which were several terminals, keyboards, and screens. A printer at the end of one table served all of them. Rachel was busily moving files from a long table against the back wall and placing them in a neat stack on another.

"Rachel, this is Mr. Larson. He's from the IRS and is looking at our inventories. Is the terminal clear?"

She stooped to pick up a file that had fallen from the table and, grasping it in one hand, used the other to shake with the IRS auditor. "Yes. Hi, Mr. Larson, I'm Rachel. Sorry about the mess."

"Looks cleaner than mine," he responded, placing his briefcase next to the keyboard. He stood next to the chair assigned to that spot. "Will I be using this one?"

"Yes, it's ready for you." She hit a keystroke that brought up the main menu. Hearing Kelly clear his throat, she excused herself to address her boss. "Just a minute, Mr. Larson. Yes, Mr. Kelly?"

"You can allow him free access. Give him the password, and let him be. It shouldn't be long." Once he had given her directions, Kelly was off.

Rachel wrote the terminal's passwords on a post-it, and stuck it on the console under the screen. "Here, what area do you wish to see first? I'll get you started."

Richard Larson sat down and was ready to enter Turner's complete system. He'd allow her to get him started, and, at the proper moment, he'd take over. It looked like a simple program and perfectly easy to navigate. "Let's go for Inventory,

Fourteen

then Purchases, then Adjustments, and, oh yes, so I don't have to bother you again, I assume you're paperless?"

"Yes, we are. Oh, we keep some backup, like check runs, but mostly, yes, we're paperless," she answered.

"In that case, point me to Journal Entries and, let's see, yes, that should be it."

She leaned over him and took control of the keyboard, hitting several keystrokes, one after another, until the screen displayed the Inventory menu. "See how easy it is?"

"Not bad. Not bad at all."

"If you get lost, hit the Help button. It's a mainframe, but it's user friendly, and the Help button works pretty well. For us dummies, you know." She stood and said, "You're on your own."

"I think I can handle it, Rachel. Oh yes, will you be close by…just in case?" This was a planned question since he knew it would be difficult to suspect him, knowing he needed her around.

He entered the keystrokes that accessed their inventory accounts and, in particular, any of those whose list of material might list the vendors who had supplied the components making up the inventoried item. Another keystroke and there it was. *SATELLITE GUIDANCE SYSTEM*, including the component parts used in its assembly. A list of vendors for each component showed him nothing that stood out—some local, some Asian, but none were familiar. So, he ended out of *PURCHASES* and entered *SALES*.

Entering *SATELLITE GUIDANCE SYSTEM*, the screen heading listed *SALES IN UNITS* for the current fiscal year. It listed only one sold, and the date sold was last month. Another keystroke and the screen displayed *CUSTOMER INFORMATION*. There it was, *TRANSCOR*.

Suddenly, he felt he was being watched. Instantly, he brought the screen back to the Purchasing menu and slowly turned as though he was about to ask Rachel a question. With his head level, he cautiously scanned the upper walls and ceiling, where he spotted a video camera in the corner between them. So as not to appear suspicious and hold his cover, he followed through with his scanning motions as if he were looking for Rachel. He thought of a question.

"Rachel, excuse me, but is there a short cut to find vendors?"

She came to his side and stood there looking at the screen. It gave him the opportunity to spot another video camera on the opposite wall. She hit Ctrl and F3, and a list of vendors filled the screen. "There you go. Anything else?"

"No. And thank you," Richard Larson replied graciously.

As long as the terminal wasn't bugged to reveal which programs he entered, he could live with the video cameras. He was convinced his cover was still intact.

She continued, "Once you hit F3, it automatically…"

He paid no attention to her directions and nodded when she asked if he understood. By then she had returned to her own desk. He brought up *TRANSCOR* in the Customer File. It showed name, address, phone, fax, buyer, and that was it. Nothing else. He brought up *MASTER CUSTOMER LIST* and the screen filled with names of countries, including Iran, Iraq, Vietnam, and Korea. It was clear to him that Turner sold its product line to countries with which the USA had some very interesting dealings, to say the least.

Ending out of *CUSTOMERS*, he entered *GENERAL LEDGER* and, specifically, *LOANS TO STOCKHOLDERS*, hoping to see a list of them. It listed one loan, and it was to Turner, himself. Not what he wanted. He thought for a second and hit a few more keys, but clearly he needed to be in another task. He ended out of *GENERAL LEDGER* and the main menu came up. He spotted one possibility and entered *LEGAL*.

A few more keystrokes, a few more screens filled with minutes of meetings and other legal stuff. More keystrokes and more legal stuff, until finally a screen appeared that was more promising, *ORIGINAL STOCK ISSUE*. He picked it, and the screen filled with the original stockholders. Just two were listed:

Kenneth Turner, President
James Fenimore, Secretary

Holy crap, he thought. James Fenimore, the president?

There he is again. He scrolled down to the bottom of the screen but that was it—only the two names. He made his mental notes and went back to the main menu.

Something about the vendor list bothered him. He wasn't sure, but normally when there's a question about credit, vendors are at the forefront. By virtue of their extension of credit, in reality they become their customers' bankers. And always, if they were smart operators, companies were indebted to their vendors. He brought up *VENDOR LIST* again and started through it. He scrolled through the *A*'s until he spotted "Amacon." He paused there. He wasn't sure why, but there was something about the name. He wrote down the address on Kirby Road in Arlington and continued scrolling until he saw something strange.

Before, he had been looking at inventories under the *ASSET REGISTER*, and now he spotted *INVENTORY* under *VENDORS*. A double-click and the full name appeared, "Inventory Service Company." It too was on Kirby Road, at the same address as Amacon. He scribbled their name next to Amacon's. He scratched his head, closed *VENDORS* and went to *GENERAL LEDGER*, where he brought up *INCOME STATEMENT* and was surprised to find an account for inventory expense. Perhaps in manufacturing, it was normal to have such an account. For the current fiscal month, only one entry appeared. It was a charge and it showed the invoice belonged to Inventory Service Company and the amount was for $22,500. It seemed like a lot of money for counting inventory. He hit *SUMMARY* and it listed ten invoices for the same amount, each for a different month in the fiscal year. For sure, it was a lot of money. A whole lot of money! He hit *PRINT* and the *SUMMARY PAGE* printed on the printer next to him. Calmly, he retrieved it, as well as a blank sheet, placing the blank sheet next to him on the desk, not anxious to alert those monitoring the video cameras, and the printed one next to his briefcase.

He stood to stretch an imaginary kink from his back and went to Rachel's side. "Excuse me again." He spoke low while rustling a piece of printer paper into a wad to muffle their conversation. "Why the inventory service? It seems a little excessive doesn't it?" He really didn't care about the amount.

He continued playing with the paper as she answered him. "On government contracts, they specify outside inventory services, third party." She returned to her work.

That was her answer, and, for now, it would have to do. He guessed she knew nothing about the entries into the general ledger and figured it was the Accounts Payable Department who had entered them. He wasn't sure if he needed to poke around any further since Accounts Payable probably wouldn't have any idea either. The only one who would know was Kelly, and he wasn't sure he wanted to risk any more time. He said his goodbye and thanked Rachel, saying he would find his own way out.

Instead, to satisfy his curiosity, he decided to look up the office of Ken Turner. He headed toward where he thought it might be.

* * * * * * * * *

Jopaq entered Turner's office on his own mission. He knew precisely the location of the CEO's office, and his research proved that Turner would be in his office that very day and at that very moment. He was in and out of Turner's office in a split second, pausing only long enough to pump a bullet from a silenced Walther 9 mm semiautomatic into Ken Turner's temple, killing him instantly as he sat at his desk.

* * * * * * * * *

A young lady pushing a cart jammed full of packages gave Richard Larson directions to Ken Turner's office. Rather than wait for an elevator for just one floor, he chose the stairs. He swung open the door, headed for the steps, but didn't see him in time. A small man dressed in coveralls was moving rapidly down the stairs from the floor above. As he rounded the corner, he met Richard Larson nearly head-on, bumping shoulders. The speeding man's tool belt contained a large black phone, such as he'd seen on the belts of telephone installers in his own hometown. The two men passed each other close enough that the phone struck Richard Larson's hand as it swung out as the other man sped past him. The telephone man nodded and smiled a hurried, but amiable, apology, and continued with haste to the lower floor. Once on the second floor, Richard Larson entered the elevator lobby, went past the elevators through a set of leaded glass doors, and into what the mail girl indicated was Turner's office. Directly inside was a small desk. It was vacant at the time. Beyond that was a private office, door slightly ajar. He walked beyond the desk to the door and pushed it open. At first, he thought he had caught the company president napping.

He cleared his throat in an attempt to let him know he was there. When it did no good, he moved closer. "Mr. Turner. Sir?"

Still, there was no response. Gale observed blood spots on the wall, and as he got closer, he saw that blood had soaked into the papers under his head. He had seen enough and, given the circumstances of his presence, decided to get out of there. As he left Turner's office, he spotted a pair of high heels poking from behind the secretary's desk. Because of the angle of his entrance, he hadn't seen them when he first came in. He'd stumbled onto a double murder.

Immediately, he flashed to the telephone installer and their chance encounter in the stairwell, but before he could consider it further, he was confronted by two security guards coming at him with arms outstretched, meaning business. They had sized up the scene in the outer office and were going for the next person in line. And, Richard Larson was it.

His timing couldn't have been worse. There was no escape. They were strong as gorillas and had him in their grasp before he was out of the dead man's office. He struggled, but it was no use. His only chance was to relax and go along peacefully, or so that's what he made them think. Amateurs that they were, thinking they had their man, they relaxed their grip for a split second. That was all he needed. Instantly, Gale raised both feet straight out in front, and with the strength and skill of an Olympic gymnast, propelled himself out of their grasp, knocking both to the floor. Quick as lightning, he hurdled over the two guards and out of the office. Soon, he was down two flights to the basement, fleeing for his life.

Gale threw open the door with a loud bang and was halfway across the basement floor by the time the door rebounded closed. As he neared another exit door on the opposite wall, the door behind him banged as the guards rushed through it. He charged through the exit door and into an alley that led to somewhere, anywhere, he didn't care, away from the gorillas. He plunged headlong through a laurel hedge and into the backyard of a neighboring restaurant, startling a couple who were in the midst of an anniversary toast.

After making some offhand comment about hedge trimmers, he scurried past the couple, through the restaurant, and onto the sidewalk, where he looked up and down the street to check out his options. Luckily, he'd parked the rental car on the street around the next corner.

He found it, got in, and accelerated toward the next stop sign, where he turned toward the Holland Tunnel and out of downtown Manhattan. He drove the car by reflex as he wondered about the telephone man and his close call with Turner's apes. Whoever wanted Turner dead had proven they wouldn't hesitate at killing anyone who got in their way. But who was he? Better yet, who was behind it besides him? It was hard enough to go against a recognizable enemy, but the unknown? Forget it. He racked his brain for clues that could explain the chance meeting of the phone man and the other encounters with the little man on the boat and, quite possibly, the man in the bar that night with Sam and Dominique.

Once in New Jersey, he looked for the nearest pay phone. He stopped at a strip mall, half of which was still under construction, where he found a pay phone. He rummaged through his pocket, looking for a quarter. He let the coin drop into the slot and dialed Senator Brewer.

"Senator, sorry to bother you. We've got to talk."

"Good to hear your voice," the senator replied. "You sound like you're out of wind. Where are you?"

Although his trust in the senator was well rooted, Gale asked himself if the senator had cronies out there somewhere? He wondered about that and the fact that his phone might be tapped. Carefully selecting every word, he continued. "I'm tied up for a while. Can we meet for drink?"

"You got it. Same time and place. It will be safe," the senator instructed.

Gale understood; they would meet at the same safe house as before. He climbed back into the car for the long drive to Washington and a short hop across the river to Arlington. It gave him the time to reconnect to past events. Dominique's story seemed true or, at least, he wanted to believe her. But he had to be careful not to mix his emotions with the facts. The blast on the waterfront; the cab driver's brains spattered on the windshield. And what about Dominique? An innocent pawn, being manipulated by Albrecht? What about Brewer? Was the senator involved in this thing more deeply than Gale had imagined? And did he allow his trust to override his hunches, which went against everything he'd learned and experienced?

Gale tried to connect the Bortens case with the senator's intelligence career but couldn't. True, he'd spent most of it in Soviet-bordered countries, like East Germany and Poland. But what had that to do with Bortens? And another thing, the senator's knowledge of the goings-on in the world of intelligence put him close to the action, even today. But still, no connection to Bortens. So far, it seemed like a dead end.

But Gale couldn't explain away the fact that the senator knew about Bortens. Too bad all the senator could tell him were bits and pieces. And, the secrecy surrounding it shouldn't have been a surprise either. After all, the intelligence business was about as sneaky as it gets. But that leads right back to Bortens. Why is Bortens a part of all this? And why couldn't the senator just simply tell him? Of course, he realized that in the inner circles of the intelligence community, the network was pretty powerful. And as much as a key player might disagree with the vote, his mere presence in that community guaranteed that he'd go with the flow or face the consequences. And, although he was just a peon back then, Gale knew all too well that the flow was powerful to the degree that it made the Mafia, at its height, look sheepish. And, once caught in the network, there wasn't much choice.

Senator Brewer was in the bar nursing a drink when Gale arrived. They shook hands like old business partners, and Gale took the empty bar stool next to the senator's. The senator must have gathered that Gale was there on business, so the formalities were kept to a minimum.

"Bill, you look hurried. Anything wrong?" asked the senator.

"That's an understatement." He motioned the waiter over. "A draft please. I don't care what kind. Anything cold."

"So, what are you coming up with?" asked the senator.

Gale figured the senator was keeping tabs on him like he did in the Company school in Langley. It irked him a little, feeling he was being fed things as the senator saw fit. But his choices were limited, so he went along with it. "Senator, please. I have a great deal of respect for you as a person. You know that."

"Yes, I do. And it's mutual, you know that too," replied the senator.

He nodded, knowing the senator was stalling. He took a gulp from the frosted mug that the waiter had placed on a fresh paper coaster. "Do you know a Ken Turner with Turner Engineering? They have a local facility here and what appears to be their financial or executive headquarters in Manhattan." He waited for the senator's response.

Senator Brewer cocked his head and bit his upper lip. "Of course, I know Ken Turner. He's a big player in Washington.

He manufactures certain equipment...for our allies. Why do you ask?"

"He's dead. Just a few hours ago."

Senator Brewer placed his forehead in his hands and shook his head slowly. He sighed heavily and regained his composure. "Ken is dead? How did it happen and where?"

"I don't have much to go on except I was there within seconds after it happened. In his Manhattan office. Funny thing, too, I think I saw the killer. Hell, we were close enough to dance."

Brewer's mouth dropped, and he froze, fumbling for words. "Can you describe him? I mean, what did he look like? Could you recognize him again if you saw him?"

"I don't think so. He was disguised. But I have the feeling that I've seen him before, and a hunch that I'll see him again."

"I don't follow you," said the senator.

"Well, let's just say he matches several guys I've seen in several encounters since I've been on this case. First of all, he's quite short—maybe five feet five, maybe less. I'm not sure. He appears to be anxious, sort of fast moving, on the go. Know what I mean? A pro!"

The senator seemed puzzled. "I don't recognize the description, right off. But listen to me, Bill. Be careful." He let his tensions go with a sigh.

Gale decided to press the senator; he suspected that somehow his old instructor wouldn't let him down. He was reliable, 100 percent committed, loyal, trustworthy, and yet fierce to his enemies—a guy Gale certainly wanted in his corner. The one thing about which he had felt certain was that if anyone had ever tried to penetrate his old friend's sector, way back when, they would certainly have met up with Brewer, not someone to mess with. He hoped it was the same now.

"Level with me. You're nervous and concerned about Turner's demise, and, I can feel it in my bones, you're anxious to tell me something. Am I right?"

The senator stared into space and slowly nodded. He looked far removed from their conversation but not far enough to be unenlightened about the facts surrounding it.

"Tell me," Gale demanded.

Senator Brewer returned to the present. "Good friend, I think it's time for you to meet someone." He motioned for the waiter to bring a phone that he plugged into an outlet in the floor under their feet. He dialed and listened, then spoke, "Brewer. Call back in one minute and talk to whoever answers. It's been swept." He pressed the button near the earpiece and placed the phone on the table between them. "Trust what you hear, but be careful. He'll identify himself as Doctor W." With that, the senator left the room.

The minute went by slowly, but he was ready when the telephone buzzed. He picked it up and said, "Yes."

The person on the other end didn't identify himself but spoke softly and cautiously. "Meet me at the Constitution Gardens near the Reflecting Pool. Come in from Constitution Avenue, between the Lincoln Memorial and Washington Monument. In one hour, and be sure you're not followed."

"One hour. I'll be there." Gale pressed the disconnect button and held it up for the waiter to retrieve.

FIFTEEN

Although Gale had no trouble following Doctor W's directions, he felt a little uneasy about the meeting. At least during daylight hours he could see whatever was coming. Nighttime was far different because it was what he couldn't see that bugged him. With modern technology, clandestine gadgets worked equally well at night. This would be the last place he would've chosen for a meeting of this sort. To make matters worse, someone else was calling the shots. Downtown would've been his choice, where microwaves would bounce from one building to another, making their private discussion incomprehensible. But, it was where Doctor W specified; therefore, he'd go along with it.

The air had a creepy stillness, and he felt like he was in a B-grade movie. He followed the path to the reflecting pond, where he spotted him. A lone man, sitting on a bench facing the pond. Looking much like a tourist on an evening stroll, Gale paused at the water's edge, looked toward the

Washington Monument, then turned away from the pond, back along the path he had just traveled, searching for any sign of being followed. Nonchalantly, he continued his search, stopping to face the Lincoln Memorial, scanning again the area behind the benches. Satisfied that he wasn't followed, he walked carefully and slowly toward the bench, eyes still searching for anything out of the ordinary.

Gale sized him up as he approached the bench. Doctor W appeared to be around sixty or so, and a fairly big man. He was wearing thick glasses that had slipped to the end of his nose. Other than a day's stubble, he was clean and wore a wrinkled overcoat, which, when he turned to greet Gale, opened to reveal a wrinkled sport coat. He slid over to make room, and patted the bench, motioning for Gale to sit next to him. His slacks were also wrinkled and stretched tight around his expanded thighs and waistline. He had chubby cheeks that puffed for air as he reset himself on the bench.

Gale sat down but didn't relax. He was still anxious about the location and wanted to make the meeting as short as possible. If he had to guess, based on his contact's attire and the stench of putrid body odor, Doctor W was on the run, probably because he knew too much about things for which he had no right to know.

"You would be Doctor W?" Gale asked.

Like a wild dog guarding his kill, Doctor W looked to the right and then to the left, leaned toward him and whispered, "Yes." While he talked, he continually moved his head from side to side, as if to scan the horizon. He fidgeted. "I understand that you're a friend of Brewer's and that you're seeking information. I can help you."

Gale was relieved that he might, at last, get some answers. He was still concerned, though, about the location, especially since Doctor W himself was stewing over himself being seen. Gale's uneasiness grew in magnitude just thinking about what the Doctor may have tucked away in the recesses of his mind—secret stuff wanted by others, he presumed. With a few people dead already and at least two others on the hit list, he didn't want to waste too much time here.

"What can you tell me about Ken Turner and Turner Engineering? The same for Daniel Seward and Transcor something-or-other," Gale asked. "And feel free to bring in President Fenimore while you're at it."

Doctor W stared at the concrete in front of the bench. He never looked Gale in the eyes again. He whispered, "Well first, Fenimore made some pretty strong commitments." He paused to look over his shoulder then continued, motioning for Gale to lean closer to hear every word.

"To whom?" Gale asked.

"He compromised our country's security. Or at least, it could do so in the future," Doctor W stated. "Well anyway, it sent the Pentagon stammering, and they're not the only ones. All the intelligence agencies, defense, national security, army, navy, air force, and the whole damn intelligence community, for that matter."

His choices of words were those of someone with experience, an unlikely match to his unkempt manner. Gale quickly got the idea that Doctor W knew what he was talking about. "Why is that?" Gale asked.

"Why?" Doctor W echoed. "Don't you know anything about what's going on around here?" He didn't allow Gale the time to reply. "It's politics, and big bucks, and along with that, big-time spooksville." He nodded in the direction of the White House. "Besides making a fortune on the sly, his only interest is in reelection. You mix that with the desires of the Pentagon to bomb a third world country and the CIA to assassinate their leader and what have you got? A bunch of turkeys running around, each carrying out their own agenda, without a clue as to the long-term effect to the country. Nobody cares, period. And that's it. And in the end, nothing of any importance happens except a few changes in foreign governments, a policy here or there, and, of course, the prime reason for it all, a whole bunch of money being pocketed by them that gets. Now I ask you, does this make any sense?"

"Well, yes and no," Gale replied. "You mentioned big bucks. What's the president's connection here?"

"Hell, man, he controls Turner," Doctor W whispered. "Turner's just a puppet in this thing. He does exactly what he's told. Make sense now?"

"Yes, I'm afraid it does," replied Gale, wondering if this new contact knew anything about Turner's unexpected departure.

"A few people with different interests, going off half-cocked in their own directions with nobody in control, no master plan, no nothing. So here's what's going on. Good thing you're sitting down. Basically if you or I did what the president did, we'd be tried for treason and our butts hung from the highest yardarms. But he, of all people, is giving our secrets away to the Saudis."

"And lining his own pocket at the same time!" said Gale.

"You got it," nodded Doctor W. "It could absolutely cripple our defense posture. Sure, once he had the ears of the Pentagon and the intelligence community to some degree, they even halfway agreed to the sale of a piece of equipment, but only if it was altered prior to shipment."

"Altered?" Gale asked.

"Yes. Altered so that it would still work but without certain components. Altered so it would be, let's say, nearly as effective as our own, but not really so."

"Nearly, you say?"

"In other words," Doctor W continued, "they would think their equipment would be on a par with ours and, lo and behold, it wouldn't be. In fact, the missing components ensured us that should a switcheroo ever happen, we'd be able to penetrate their restricted areas without being noticed. Pretty slick."

"Switcheroo?" asked Gale

"Things change, my good man. Things change. For instance, should the Chinese outbid us in the oil market, different laws of economics kick in, and so will the Saudis' strategies. They don't give a flying rat's butt about us. The Arabs would just as easily buy their chicken noodle soup in Beijing. And when cars stop burning gas, who's going to give a damn about the camel herders?"

"I see," said Gale. "So, what happened with the system?"

"So what happened is this. The system Fenimore sold them, the one Turner designed and built, was the real deal. It had all the real-deal components. And, it left our defenses wide open. Hell, man, if push came to shove, there would be no way we could penetrate that system without being spotted. Worse yet, our missiles would be spotted the second they left our air space. Not a good deal for us."

"I find it difficult to believe that one man, even our president, has the power to make such a deal, don't you?" Gale asked.

"Why?" asked Doctor W. "Good God, man, the guy's got the balls of an elephant and the brain to boot. He's got so many guys kissing his butt, he just picks one with the connections and the deal's done. It's simple."

"I guess, if you say so."

"I say so? It's not me saying so. It's what is!" shouted Doctor W, who by then had puffed his chest out, proud of what he knew but sick that he had to tell it to a stranger. He realized his voice had raised and looked around to see if he'd been seen, then settled down.

"So—"

"So, he sold us out," declared Doctor W.

"One thing bothers me," said Gale. "What's so unusual about this system, this guidance system?"

"Unusual? I'll tell you what's so unusual," explained Doctor W. "The damn thing has two unique features that, as I said, weren't supposed to be attached to that particular system, which was a detection system, pure and simple. But no, this one had a feature that could jam the frequencies of the other guy's missiles prior to take off, making it impossible to launch. Second, it could take over a launched missile and guide it to any chosen destination, most probably back to its own point of origin—satellite, surface, shipboard, or aircraft. It doesn't matter."

"That's some system," Gale commented.

"The Pentagon. That's who's really upset about it. Oh sure, the CIA's in a dither, but not like the Pentagon. Hell, the president's out of control and they can't do a damn thing about it."

"I think they're trying," Gale interjected.

"How so?" Doctor W whispered, keeping a watchful eye.

"Haven't you heard about the original system being lost at sea?"

"Oh yes. I've heard, but it only slows up the pace a little. It doesn't take much to build another one. They're hot off the assembly line, you know."

"But Ken Turner's no longer in the picture. He's been killed."

At the mention of Turner's death, Doctor W showed no emotion but, instead, continued whispering. "He's just the owner, the designer. They can do it without him. No problem. How did he meet his demise by the way?"

Gale described what he saw at Turner Engineering, including his run-in with the telephone installer. At that point, he had Doctor W's complete attention.

"I think the Pentagon has some help here," commented Doctor W. "There's a professional assassin out there, a real mechanic from Europe or Asia, I don't know where. But I know of him There are at least ten governments, including both Iran and Iraq, that are after him. The Mossad would kill him on sight. If I could make an educated guess, I'd say someone, not the foreigners I mentioned, paid him a ton of cash, but someone right here, who wanted to use his talents. It was a professional hit. Of course, you know that."

"Attempts have been made on me as well—"

"This is a big one." Doctor W interrupted, not the slightest bit interested in Gale's run-in with the assassin. "Only a select few are involved."

"Can you mention any names? I'd be grateful," Gale asked, his eyes fixed to the concrete.

Again Doctor W made several looks around, then leaned over to whisper, "Talk to Cavalli, head of the CIA; then talk to the president. Good luck on that one. Then go to the Senate and look up—"

Suddenly, Doctor W's body heaved forward as the front of his head exploded, spraying blood, brains, and pieces of skull to the concrete in front of the bench. His body hit the concrete full force, and came to rest about six feet away. Gale quickly crawled under the bench for protection and winced as he saw a silent flash of light from the parking lot. A second bullet shattered the back of the bench. He was a sitting duck and needed to make a quick move or face the same fate as Doctor W.

He sprang to his feet and darted to the closest tree, gun drawn, waiting for another flash. He peered from the safety of the tree to see a man running across the parking lot toward the street beyond. He took off in hot pursuit about fifty yards shy of the shooter, who by this time had reached Independence Avenue, where he got into a car and sped off.

Gale reached his car and followed the shooter across the Roosevelt Memorial Bridge and north up the Potomac River to Chesterbrook, outside of Arlington, south of CIA's Langley complex. The lead car was in no hurry, so the shooter must have assumed he wasn't followed. The car stopped next to a warehouse. Gale hit the lights and pulled over a few hundred feet away. The shooter walked to the front door where he bent over and paused. He stayed in that position until the door finally opened. He entered without turning on the lights.

Gale assumed that the shooter had picked the lock. Unsure as to his whereabouts within the building, he crept closer, darting from bush to bush, keeping a close lookout for shadows or figures in any of the building's windows. Spotting a tree close to the front door, he went for it, his gun clenched in his fist. He snapped out the cylinder to check its contents. Satisfied, he shook the gun enough to snap the cylinder back home, and returned it to the holster.

A hunch told him that in his haste, the shooter may not have locked the door in case a quick exit were required. He was right. Gale slipped in quietly and headed for cover within the office. Except for a single dimly lit computer screen, the office was dark. He listened but heard nothing, so he sat down at the computer and attempted to log into the screen but was blocked when he couldn't come up with a password.

He rifled through a basket filled with papers, when suddenly he found a file folder, marked "Eyes-Only." He stuffed it inside his shirt and stealthily, he crawled to the door leading from the office to the warehouse and edged it open without making a sound. Still in a crouch, he eased himself through the door opening and into the warehouse. He returned the door to its half-closed position and crept slowly and silently down a dark corridor that ran for fifty feet or so. The tiled floor was littered and broken. The walls were covered with graffiti. The ceiling was a tangle of old electric wires and cables with infrequent bare light bulbs. Water dripped into a large puddle in one corner. It smelled damp and musty.

Suddenly, he was hit from behind, but the blow missed its mark and caught him between his shoulder blades. He hit the wall forcefully. With a high-pitched yell, Gale pushed off the wall and tackled his attacker. In the last instant before making contact, he saw the gun coming from beneath the man's lapel, but Gale collided with him before the gun was put into action. The force of Gale's momentum carried both of them onto a large table. The table tipped, sending both sprawling to the floor.

Gale's only interest was the gun. As he and his attacker rolled around the floor, Gale managed to grab the man's wrist. The gun went off, sending a bullet into a wall behind him. His opponent took advantage of his superior speed, and flipped Gale over his shoulder. Gale hit the floor with a thud. Pain dashed through his right side as he rolled to the right to avoid being kicked. He bounced to his feet and in a crouched position, made himself ready for the next attack. He had lost sight of him and, before he could react, was struck from behind. He heard someone laugh, then the laughter faded away.

* * * * * * * * *

Fifteen

Jopaq could have killed his opponent on the spot but, instead, chose his other alternative. Paid to eliminate targets who stand in the way of his clients' successes, for now he considered the unconscious adversary sprawled on the concrete before him an opponent, not a target, worthy of staying alive. Jopaq subscribed to the theory that if he eliminated his opponents, his fighting would be over. So, to perpetuate his business, he allowed Gale to live, to fight him another day, and, most important, to ensure continued employment. He let the building burn to destroy all traces of him being there.

* * * * * * * * * *

Gale heard a faint sound of a car starting as he attempted to open his eyes. His eyelids were too heavy, and his first inclination was to sleep. The room became distant—someone was in the room, then he was not; it was all in slow motion. That was all he remembered until the foul smell of gasoline and burning wet rags jarred him back to his senses. The building was ablaze.

Flames leaping toward the ceiling surrounded him. He saw an opening. As the flames spread toward a concrete barrier offering nothing to fuel the hungry blaze, they shot straight up toward the ceiling. He flattened himself against the concrete barrier and inched his way toward a window at the end of the corridor. He placed his jacket over his head and shoulders, and hurdled through the window, spraying glass and pieces of windowpane everywhere. He hit the ground, rolled through the debris, and slammed against a fence post, where he lay motionless for a few seconds, unaware for a split second where he was and how he got there. Fearful he was hurt, he slowly began to wiggle his toes and fingers, then his legs and arms, until he got up on one knee and then stood, surveying the rest of his body. Outside of a few glass splinters embedded in his jacket, and other than a few cuts and bruises, he was unhurt. Then it came back to him. He ran to the front of the building only to see taillights in the distance quickly accelerating. The air was filled with the dust from spinning tires in the gravel parking lot.

Gale reached his car, slammed it into reverse, and spun the tires as he backed into a small tree. He hit drive and sprayed gravel and dust behind him as he reached the pavement, squealing his tires as he picked up speed. He hit eighty and still no sign of the car. He pushed it to the floor, hitting a hundred, and finally he saw a set of taillights far ahead. When he reached an effective following distance, he lightened up on the throttle and kept a constant speed, ensuring he wouldn't lose him. He hoped this was the right car. It turned into another parking lot, this time a nicely paved one, and came to a stop. Before Gale reached the scene, the driver was gone, presumably into the building. He'd almost forgotten about the file. Luckily, through the excitement the file remained stuffed into his trousers behind his shirt. He retrieved it and laid it on the front seat next to him. Rather than chance being spotted, he parked on the street and went the rest of the way on foot.

He quietly stepped to the front landing and placed his ear against the door. He smelled fresh paint. His face was against a freshly painted sign. He paid no attention to what it read, but he heard talking—at least two men. He strained to hear but the door was too thick for any clear sounds to penetrate. He tried the outside wall, but it, too, allowed no discernible sounds to escape the interior of the building. He slipped around the corner to the shadows, where he spotted a window. He found an empty cable spool, slid it next to the window, and hopped up, slowing raising his head until he could see inside. It was dark, but the window was open an inch. He sized it up and believed it led to an unoccupied room.

Cautiously, he pried on it until it was fully opened, praying that it hadn't been alarmed. His ample biceps gently lifted his massive frame to the window's edge, where he pivoted his legs up and inside the window without making a sound. It looked like a parts supply room. Rows of steel shelving were filled with cardboard bins, on the fronts of which were written part numbers for the items supposedly contained within. The workbench had a vise in front of every stool, and one soldering gun for every work station was hanging on a pegboard running the length of the bench. One vise held an electronic component of some type.

He closed the window to ensure that, from the outside, his entry would be unnoticed and, more importantly, so that a freak gust of wind wouldn't force the door ahead of him to either open more quickly than he'd planned or close behind him as he went through it. After he'd felt the wrath of his attacker, he wanted no repeats.

The two men's voices were louder and nearly understandable. If he could just open the door a crack, their voices would be more audible. He decided to try it. Their voices were clear enough to make out most of the conversation.

The one doing the talking was in the middle of a sentence and clearly upset. There was anger in his voice and he was demanding action.

"...this is getting out of hand. You'd best damn well clean up this situation and do it now. We've got other things pending, but this needs completion before we can proceed."

The other spoke a dialect Gale couldn't detect— German? Asian? Not sure, but he spoke clearly and precisely for someone out of wind. "I have good understanding and fully appreciate the situation. I ask you to trust me...please...I will take care of it."

"Were you followed?" asked the one obviously in charge.

"Nein," replied the other. "I was not followed,"

There was a strong sense of urgency in his voice. "We brought you here to help clean up a tricky situation. You were most helpful in other skirmishes and, quite frankly, that is why we had that conversation and why we have sweetened your Cayman account. We've fulfilled our end of the deal. Can we anticipate anything other than that from you? I mean after the miscalculations?"

"Now wait a moment. The most important target is down. Very good?" Jopaq knew that his opponent was down, but certainly not out.

"Hold it," Adams interrupted, "that's only one part of the deal. I realize we hadn't counted on outside interference, but the fact that you accepted our offer on an open-ended basis means just that. There's more work to be done."

"Herr Adams, I realize that, and, if you'll please be patient, the agreement will be consummated, as you anticipated."

Gale couldn't recall hearing the name Adams. He kept listening. He was getting anxious, now that a name had been mentioned. But he had to remain cautious and not be detected.

"I hadn't anticipated so many dead bodies," said Adams. "Our original agreement called for just the plane."

"But Mein Herr, events have become altered, and please remember, I am here to help."

"Point well taken," Adams acquiesced. "And, please understand, we are appreciative, just a little nervous. I can tell you this. If this damnable piece of equipment ever gets into the Saudis' hands, it's going to be a cold day in hell. Your new job is to make sure it doesn't, no matter what. I don't care who you have to neutralize, but it can't happen. Is that understood?"

"Yes yes, very good…absolutely."

"Good," Adams responded. "And by the way, we hadn't counted on the outside interference becoming so, shall we say, nosey."

"Ja, that was taken care of just moments ago," Jopaq replied, knowing full well that he allowed his adversary to live.

The man's words shook Gale to the bone. He was believed to be dead at this very moment, not really knowing that his life had been spared. And in the next room, just a few feet away, was his would-be killer. He fought back the urge to slam the door open, shove his gun up his ass, and pull the trigger. But the only purpose it would have served was his own, certainly not that of the assignment. He needed the other man's name.

"Just make certain that it's taken care of," ordered Adams. "That would wind up our problems, and you would be free to return home. By the way, do you think the FAA would have—"

"Please, Herr Adams, but the only person to modify the report is now eliminated," interrupted the other man. "As it stands, pilot error and acts of God contributed equally. You are in the clear. Others who might know are likewise written out of the script."

"Except?" asked Adams.

"Well Ja, one exception—"

"It might be necessary. We will advise on that one."

It sounded like the conversation was coming to a close, so Gale's first instinct was to rush in and grab the two of them. However, his previous encounter left him a little wary of handling two, let alone, the one. He was sure they wouldn't enter the parts room, so he remained to catch every word.

"We would like to see samples of the gas canisters and their triggering device, that is, if you would care to offer them for sale. We're always looking for other alternatives," said Adams.

"Ja, that can be arranged," said the other man. "When this is over, perhaps we can meet in, say, The Hague where the items could be presented to you."

"Yes, we'll certainly look at them after this is complete. Now, if you will excuse me, I have a game to attend."

Gale heard two sets of footsteps, a door open and close, and that was it. Silence. He waited for a few moments until the two cars started and drove off. When he was sure they were gone, he opened the door and stood where seconds before, the two men were engaged in a conversation that he wished he could've recorded. The overhead light was still on, and from what he guessed, it must have been a night light. Before moving into the office too far, he scanned the walls and ceiling for any signs of an alarm system. Spotting none, he continued, looking for signs of anything he thought would be important to his mission. The room was an office, nothing more.

He opened one of the desk drawers to find it empty. So was the one next to it. His instincts were working overtime. He opened the side drawers and they, too, were empty. Just as he thought, all the desks were empty. The place was like a movie set without cameras. Nothing made much sense. Not one stick of evidence or anything that would lead him anywhere. What he heard from behind the door would have to do.

He had one thing. Although he was missing a face, he had the name of Adams. Hopefully it would lead him to the identity of the mystery hit man. He unlocked the dead bolt, and as he opened the door inward and stepped over the threshold, he caught the aroma of lacquer he had smelled a few minutes earlier. A sign had just been painted on the door. He stepped back to where he could read "AMACON

ELECTRIC." Once inside the car, he picked up the cell phone and dialed the senator.

* * * * * * * * *

It was early the next morning when the director of the CIA was seated at his desk examining a stack of files, first looking through the top one, setting it aside face down, then taking the next, and so on. To his secretary, who said he had a visitor, Dean Cavalli said he'd be a few minutes longer.

Impatient and anxious, Adams paced the floor outside the director's office. He was ready to explode. The secretary apologized, and said it would be a long day today. Finally, the director instructed his secretary to show Adams in.

Without so much as a good morning, Adams walked to the side of the director's desk. "Dean, this is getting out of hand."

Cavalli still had his nose stuck in one of the files, about a third of the way from the top and didn't bother looking up. His reading glasses were at the tip of his nose. "Uh huh. So what's the problem, Allen?" he asked, then finally acknowledged him.

"Damn it Dean, this is important. We've got a maniac running loose out there and no telling who's next. It's out of our control." Allen Adams, the president of Amacon Electric, was making his point.

"Calm yourself, for God's sake, and have a seat," Cavalli directed.

Fifteen

Adams continued to pace the spacious office, then stopped at the far end where he turned to face Cavalli. "Do you have any idea what's going on? You should. You're the director of the CIA, or did you forget?"

By this time, Adams had Cavalli's full attention. Cavalli removed his glasses and placed them, folded, on the stack of unexamined files. He rubbed the bridge of his nose with the fingers of both hands then held them in front of his eyes to examine the oil on his fingers. He rubbed his hands together, then stretched his arms out in front, and finally brought his hands together on the desk, folded in front of him. "Brief me."

By now, Adams was standing behind one of the leather chairs opposite the director's desk. He leaned forward, both hands supporting his tall frame. "I'll brief you, OK. Then I want some support. This is your game, you know—"

"Don't you play that with me," Cavalli interrupted. "You're a part of this as well as anybody. Besides, you know as well as I that the real loose cannon is the one in the Oval Office."

"All right then, what's next?" Adams asked, finally relaxing and taking a seat in the leather chair, facing the director. He crossed his legs and unbuttoned an expensive sport coat.

"You're our connection in this whole thing, Allen. Hell, Amacon hires the mechanic, it orchestrates the hits, and what's more, it controls the cleanup committee. That's the agreement between you and the Company. Besides, you're well paid for what you do—a budget, I might add, that's not approved by the Company...or by Fenimore."

"Don't leave me hanging out there," Adams pleaded.

"We'll take care of the politics. My position is that I don't know what you're doing and don't want to. That's another part of the agreement, just as you wish to know nothing about this end. Am I correct in that, Allen? Allen?"

Adams was thinking. "That is correct. Yes, it's the way we agreed. But, hear me out. We have an intruder, nosing around and causing some real concern. He's getting information from someone within our ranks."

Cavalli perked up. "Within our ranks? How do you mean?"

"I mean, we've got ourselves a mole. A big one, right in our midst."

"OK, I'll break the rules. You tell me about what I don't wish to know, and maybe I'll share with you some political goings-on." Cavalli grew more agitated, but tried to calm himself down.

"An intruder has made himself known in a couple of instances," Adams stated. "First, he shows up in court with Bortens's attorney. Albrecht thought he was a part of their legal team, but it turns out he's not."

"So, forget him for a minute. Finish your story."

Adams continued. "We know why the plane went down, and we thought we had it covered."

"You mean Wilson?" asked Cavalli.

"I doubt if he got the chance to cash his check."

"Explain that one."

"His report on FAA letterhead pretty much set the blame on Bortens's pilots. Pilot error. But, Bortens's lady was ready to testify otherwise, so, as you know, Albrecht paid her a visit."

"And?"

"And, just that. He made her an offer, and she needed cash, so they struck a deal for her to recant her testimony and tell it like it was. Or let's say how we wanted it to be."

"So, everything was going OK?"

"Yes, until the next day in court where she screwed up our plans and testified that everything was hunky-dory, and that something else must have caused the crash. Well, as you know, that opened a big one. So, fearful of Wilson going with the flow, Jopaq, our great mechanic, paid him a visit. So, that part's taken care of. Now, it seems like our intruder is going even further, getting information from someone we've all partied with. Who? God only knows."

"How deep does this thing go, Allen?" asked Cavalli.

"Pretty darn deep. Again, as you know, Fenimore was putting pressure on Turner to make another system, so Jopaq paid Turner a visit as well. With him out of the way, no system. At least that's what someone thinks. And, that's where our man ran headlong into the intruder, whoever he is. And it gets even more interesting."

"Allen, hold it a minute. What about Inventory Service Company? They were keeping an eye out in Turner's operation? What happened there?"

"True, I had ISC infiltrate their operations," explained Adams. "But even they became caught up in the daily grind and soon became ineffective. Actually, no, I take that back. It wasn't that they were ineffective. Nothing was going on. So, they became complacent and relaxed. I doubt that it made any difference anyway since all we were doing was making assurances that certain house jobs were given priority. There was nothing we could have done, overtly at least, to stop him from sending that system, or sending another for that matter. No, there was nothing we could have done to prevent Turner's demise. It was inevitable if we were to stop production permanently. Oh, that reminds me."

"Of what?" asked Cavalli.

"There's been a guy running around Washington, trying to make money by selling out old friends, getting into certain political offices or anywhere else to steal and deal in secret information. A real slimeball."

"I've heard of him, been around for a while," said Cavalli. "Calls himself Doctor W. No match in our files but, apparently, a friend of somebody higher up. Anyway, continue."

"Well, it seems that this guy, Doctor W or whoever he is, knows a bit about some inner circle goings-on. So we put a tail on him and found out he lives pretty much in the streets, or at least that's what we think. It wasn't all that easy locating him. But once we were on him, we kept on him. At first we thought he was harmless and, maybe, was selling secrets that were too old to be of any use to anybody. But then he was spotted within the walls of the Senate and the House and different places in and around the Capitol. He was even spotted in line at one of the White House tours. Now, why would an old salt, like him, take a guided tour through the White House?"

"It's getting more interesting every minute," commented Cavalli.

"It's only the beginning," said Adams. "The guy is so paranoid that he walks around in circles, looking for spooks behind every tree. I'm not sure he hasn't bumped into a few telephone poles, looking the other way. Well, anyway, he spent a lot of time in a phone booth, and our tail had a hunch. So, we nabbed Jopaq and told him to neutralize what might be a new situation."

"And?"

"And, he did," said Adams. "Except he was in a meeting with the so-called intruder."

"Now hold everything, Allen, just a minute. You mean with all our means at hand, you haven't identified the intruder? Come on."

"Jopaq is the only one who has had any contact, and he thought he'd put the guy down for good."

"Oh yes, the fire?" asked Cavalli.

"I'm not sure it worked," said Adams. "At least, I'm not counting on it. The guy is made of iron. If he survived the rocket blast, he may have made it through the fire. That rocket deal, by the way, was a surprise to us too.

"What about the lawyer?"

"Nothing's been reported," replied Adams. "I doubt if he made it. He was right in the middle of the blast zone. I'm surprised the broad and the other guy made it out of there alive. His assignment was to get her, but our mechanic has a one-track mind—he could care less about collateral damage. But he's damned good."

"Is that so?" Cavalli questioned Adams.

"Well, I'm not making excuses, and he did foul up on our intruder. But, he's assured me that the next time will be the last."

"Getting back to Doctor W," Cavalli said.

Adams uncrossed one leg and crossed the other. He took a deep breath and let it out quickly. "Our mechanic took care of him. Whatever secrets he had stuffed away in his fat little head were sprawled over the sidewalk."

"And so, who is next on your little hit list?"

"My hit list?" stammered Adams. "You'd better take some ownership of this deal."

"Calm down, Allen, everything's going to work out just fine," reassured Cavalli.

"So, we don't know what's next. The guy's got connections we don't know about. We think he's part of the Bortens team. That's about all."

"You'd better follow up on it," Cavalli recommended. "You know as well as I how important this is. If we have a leak, we'd better damn well find it. And I mean now. If you have to, reassess your position with the mechanic and up the ante."

"He's being paid quite enough," said Adams.

"Is there anything else we should go over?" asked Cavalli.

"What about the president?"

"What about him?" asked Cavalli.

"Just what I said, what about the president?"

SIXTEEN

It was another typical late fall day in the Capitol city, which meant temperatures wouldn't reach much above the fifties. Winter was quickly settling in. The day started out overcast, but the forecast called for afternoon sun, perfect for the tourists, who couldn't wait to board their buses and be off to yet another monument.

As Gale walked along the sidewalk, a tour bus whizzed by and came to an abrupt stop a few feet in front of him. As the air brakes hissed, the door opened, and the first pair of camera-toting tourists was off the bus and proceeding up the steps to see if Lincoln's statue matched the photos in their high-school history books.

Senator Brewer stood at the base of the steps, one foot resting on a higher step, legs spread comfortably apart, one hand in his pants pocket and the other holding a morning paper. Upon seeing Gale, Brewer turned toward a park bench and motioned for him to follow. The senator sat at the far end of the bench, and Gale joined him. A century-old cherry tree stood majestically behind the bench.

Gale crossed his legs and clasped his hands around his knee, rocking slightly until his back rested against the park bench. "I need your help," he insisted.

The senator ran his hand through a head of graying, bushy hair while his deep-set eyes showed concern over Gale's insistence over their prompt meeting. "I'll do what I can. What in particular?"

Another busload of tourists had unloaded at the curb and mingled around the grounds. A teenage girl focused her camera on a boyfriend with the memorial as a backdrop. One particular tourist sidestepped between them, nodding an excuse-me as he did. The brim of an expensive straw hat added credibility, as did the two cameras hanging from his neck.

Gale responded to Senator Brewer. "Well, first, thanks for your help. The ID worked well. It got me in and helped me discover some very interesting information which, quite frankly, I'm puzzled about."

"How so?" asked the Senator.

"I followed a very remarkable person to a couple of different places," Gale said, saying only enough to get the senator's attention. "First there was this isolated warehouse in suburban Chesterbrook." He paused to see any changes in the senator's expression, but there were none. "I tried to get into one of their computer terminals but couldn't, not that I'm surprised. All I got was a message saying, 'ACCESS DENIED.' Does that make any sense to you?"

* * * * * * * * *

Sixteen

As Gale and Senator Brewer talked, the tourist with the two cameras scanned the area with one. He moved nonchalantly around the grounds, an impeccably dressed tourist, beneath whose ordinary exterior prowled a lethal and calculating assassin. Blending in with the crowd, he appeared to have a genuine interest in Lincoln's abolishment of slavery, but only he was aware of his blatant disregard for anything pure and moral.

* * * * * * * * * *

The senator responded to Gale's inquiry. "Let me think about it. Nothing comes to me right away, but go on."

"Then I made it to an office building not far away from the warehouse, again in Chesterbrook, not far from our old stomping grounds."

Other than tightening his jaw, the senator showed no other response. "And?"

"The name on the front door was Amacon Electric. Know anything about it?"

The senator replied, "Name's not familiar, but give me that error message or whatever it was that came up on the screen."

Gale repeated, "'ACCESS DENIED.' But that's not all. I found a file, marked 'Eyes-Only.'" Gale handed the file folder to Senator Brewer.

"I can tell you this much. That particular phrase is used by the Company to mean Top Secret. Except that—"

"Except what?" Gale demanded.

"It's a classification that really doesn't mean top secret, in the normal sense of the word. Anyone with proper clearance could access whatever it was that someone felt should be top secret. And, it's more than that. It's a code word meaning it's restricted even further." The senator was searching for the right words.

"Senator, are you going to tell me or not?"

"Eyes-Only," replied Senator Brewer. "Like this file says."

"Whose eyes?" Gale demanded. "The file doesn't say who it's meant for."

"Only one." The senator drew in a deep breath and slowly let it out.

"OK. I'm waiting."

* * * * * * * * * *

Jopaq was closing in. His high cheekbones touched the bottom frame of his dark sunglasses perched high atop a large, sharp nose. His breathing grew more responsive as the need for additional adrenaline spurred him onward, stalking his prey. He worked his away around the base of Lincoln's Memorial, half on and half off the steps. A few more steps and he would have them in view. This time, he wouldn't fail.

* * * * * * * * * *

As Senator Brewer mulled it over, Gale scanned the crowd but found nothing out of the ordinary. Except for one person.

Gale noted the tourist's camera right away. It had a long, telephoto lens, and it was aimed at both him and Senator Brewer. There was something else. The long lens wasn't reflecting any sunlight. In fact, Gale could make out the lens itself—it had no glass in it. A quick flashback to his CIA days, and it came to him.

The tourist hesitated for a split second that gave Gale the time he needed to draw his revolver and explode a bullet into the tourist's leg. But it was too late. The tourist had already pressed the shutter release, propelling a high velocity, small-caliber bullet directly into the chest of Senator Kent Brewer. Gale's first reaction was to go after him, but he figured he wouldn't get too far before being picked up by security. His second reaction was the right one. His friend needed him more.

Instantly, he was down on all fours, cradling the senator's near-lifeless body in his arms, supporting his head on his chest. He reached his arm around the senator's back and felt a warm oozing on the jacket, which told him that the bullet went completely through his body. Gale knew in an instant that his friend, who had been a mother hen to him for all these years, wouldn't make it. Suddenly Senator Brewer's eyes opened, and he uttered, "My eyes, Bill. I'm the one."

Even in his final moments, Senator Brewer saw the confusion in Gale's expression. "Come closer," he whispered. As Gale did, the senator continued. "Please see that the deal goes through."

"But I thought—"

"I'm sorry to have deceived you, my friend," the senator whispered. "All along I've played both sides...but please...Fenimore is right..." Senator Brewer closed his eyes and quietly slipped away.

It hit him like a ton of bricks, and yet, the senator's final words were a bit of a relief for Gale. All along, he had suspected that his old friend was a key player on the wrong side, and he was saddened over it. Now he was sure that the CIA was acting not in the best interest of the country. But in whose? he wondered, as he came to his senses about leaving before he was discovered.

Carefully, but quickly, he eased the senator's head down to the soft, green grass, then picked himself up, and turned to walk away. As he did, he took one more glance over his shoulder to the lifeless body of Senator Brewer and whispered, "Keep you head down, old friend." Gale was gone before the police arrived.

The early morning drive back to Manhattan gave him the quiet time to reflect on the bizarre events that had enveloped him in a deep cover situation. He replayed them all, from the courtroom to Dominique's abduction, the explosion and her nearly dying in his arms, to the near misses on their lives. He went over the assassination of Doctor W, the chases, his near-death encounter at the warehouse, the overheard conversation between the hit man and a guy named Adams, and finally full circle to his friend, Senator Brewer.

He had to hand it to the tourist. With a .357 slug in his leg and still able to get off a round into the senator, he was good. And the worst part about it, he was still out there. Gale took the cell phone from the glove box and dialed the hotel. He felt a sudden hunger for Dominique's closeness and wished the drive would go more quickly. The phone only rang twice.

Sixteen

She burst into tears as she heard his voice and stuttered between sobs, "Oh Bill, I'm so glad you are OK. The television news said—"

"I know. I'm fine." He felt a rush of emotion swelling inside him. "I'm on my way and should be there in a few hours."

"Please be careful," Dominique warned.

"I know. I've got to meet with the judge and get this whole thing straightened out." The Brewer surprise still haunted him, but he kept it to himself. "Oh yes, is Sam around?"

"He's in San Francisco," she replied. "Can I call him for you?"

"Yes, you can. Get in touch with him right away and have him call Judge Rickey and authorize me to speak on Bortens's behalf. It's very important, and Sam will have to trust me on this. Can you do that for me?"

"As soon as we're done, I'll call him. I'm certain that it'll be fine." Dominique paused then continued. "Oh Bill, I forgot to tell you. He was found floating in the Long Island Sound."

Gale asked, "Who was found floating and why?"

"Albrecht," she replied. "From the explosion they say."

Hearing that, he felt more at peace. He placed the cell phone in the passenger seat, and accelerated to keep up with traffic. He reached for the cell phone again and asked directory assistance to connect him to Judge Thomas Rickey in New York City.

"Hello, Your Honor, this is Bill Gale, representing Bortens. Do you remember?"

The voice on the other end was judicious and firm, but friendly. "Yes, Mr. Gale, of course."

"I have some very crucial information relating to the Bortens matter and am on my way from Washington to see you. Sam Rader will be calling you within the next hour or so to advise you that I may speak on their behalf. Can you leave some time for me late this afternoon?"

"I'll be in court the rest of the day, but when you arrive, go to my chambers, and tell my secretary that I am expecting you. If we need more time, we can set it for tomorrow. Is that sufficient, Mr. Gale?"

"Absolutely, sir. I should be in your office no later than four this afternoon. And, sir, thank you for your patience in all of this. What I have to say will set the record straight and help settle this once and for all."

Again, he cut the power and set the phone on the passenger seat. He could relax for now. Bortens was off the hook. He pulled the car into the hotel's valet parking area and told the young man he was in for the evening. Rather than see Dominique, though, he headed for his appointment with Judge Rickey. It was four thirty, and he hoped the judge would still see him.

Judge Rickey's secretary was sitting at her desk as usual, entering data into a computer terminal. She looked up as Gale entered and gave him a cordial smile.

"Good afternoon. I'm Bill Gale, representing Bortens. The judge is expecting me. He said that if you—"

"I'll get him for you," she interrupted and, in seconds, was through the door leading to his courtroom. Soon she returned and escorted Gale into the judge's private office, where she offered him a seat.

Within a few moments, Judge Rickey came through the door, extended his hand, and sat on the corner of his desk. His black robe was still neat after a day on the bench. Even in a judge's robe, he was smartly dressed and handsome, and his hair was freshly styled. His wide eyes searched for the truth as he dropped his round jaw and parted his thin lips to speak. "Mr. Gale, it's good to see you. I was a little concerned about Miss Fabours and, to be honest with you, about Mr. Rader as well as the entire Bortens organization. It's very seldom that we find a recant in our court. Especially on this level. So, whatever you have to tell me, I hope it's favorable."

Gale quickly summarized. "It's not only favorable but it completely exonerates Bortens. In fact, this particular situation runs so deep that Bortens was simply a pawn in a scheme so bizarre that it's hard to believe."

Gale told the judge the entire story, including the attempts on his and Dominique's lives and the assassinations of Turner, his secretary, Senator Brewer, Doctor W, and the cab driver and the kidnap encounter between Dominique and Albrecht. He kept certain facts to himself, as eyes-only, such as Senator Brewer's playing both sides. It had nothing to do with the case, yet everything to do with the country's security.

He summarized by saying, "Your Honor, this thing goes a lot higher than you could imagine. All the way up to the highest levels of our government, including the president, himself."

Judge Rickey stood and realigned a gold pen set that had been pushed a few inches from center. "That is, indeed, quite a story." He walked around to his chair and sat down. "What sort of proof do you have, Mr. Gale?

"Your honor, I can only offer you a certain portion of the facts, and ask you to trust that Bortens has been an innocent pawn in this whole thing. This goes so deep into so many political corners, that I must maintain the data's confidentiality."

Judge Rickey paused in thought, then gave his decision. "It's true, Mr. Gale, that the court is not interested in the other data to which you refer. And, since what you and Miss Fabours tell me gives me reasonable doubt, the decision will go to Bortens."

"Thank you, Your Honor—"

"And," Judge Rickey added, "the court wishes to extend its thanks for all your hard work and efforts. I had a feeling that something more was involved. I shall instruct Mr. Rader to submit the necessary documentation, and this matter shall be settled. They and their insurance carrier will handle the customary liability issues with the deceased crew's families, as is normal. But I'll dismiss the civil suit and notify the plaintiff of my decision."

As he drove to the hotel, Gale couldn't help but feel awestruck by the shenanigans played by the country's highest officials. As much as he wanted to blow the whistle, he figured that nobody much cared, certainly those who ran the country. He tried to put it out of his mind but couldn't.

Sixteen

Visions of clandestine meetings circled his mind—Doctor W sneaking through underground parking decks, popping amphetamines as he lurked in the shadows, stretching his neck to peer around a giant pillar, while just a few yards away, crouched beside a van, the senator waited with a fistful of dollars for information that would later be disseminated as the hottest news in the underground movement of the country's heretofore best kept secrets.

He first turned sick at the thought of the involvement of his old friend, the senator, then caught himself. No, his old friend was, indeed, on the right side. But the way he died—not the way a spy should die. It was supposed to come on foreign soil, in some hillside of Russia or in a back alley of East Berlin. Certainly not at the base of the Lincoln Memorial.

What was he thinking? This was reality. There was no more East Berlin, and secrets were traded much more easily, with the wide use of computers and other electronic media available to every kid on the block. As for the CIA, while as much as the other members of the community liked to believe their activities were confined only to foreign soil, much was still carried on domestically, much to the annoyance of the FBI. But he had to lay it to rest. His job differed only slightly from that of the senator. At least his was in the corporate environs. But then, the more he thought about it, this particular assignment brought him back into it. He traveled a fine line.

Government can't work in a vacuum, and the same goes for big business. What dollars weren't extracted from the taxpayers were fed to the government machinery by the corporate giants and foreign entities, anxious to play in America's giant marketplace, whether aboveboard or not. The switch he'd made from government to business espionage really wasn't so different after all. Instead of penetrating a foreign government to neutralize an attack, his targets were aggressive corporations that had penetrated the networks of his clients who, rather than do their own research, took the easy road, buying what they needed. Trade secrets, exclusive formulas, customer lists, it was all for the taking.

But in Gale's case, most targets found that they hadn't thought it through completely. They hadn't figured on him being in the way. And, so far, he was batting a thousand.

He parked at the curb and nodded at the valet as he entered the hotel lobby. He picked up the key and took the elevator to his floor. The lights were off when he came in, and he felt a pang of disappointment. He had hoped Dominique would be standing there in a flimsy see-through holding out her hands, longing for his embrace. But she'd fallen asleep on the bed, under a thin spread, watching the early evening news, which was still on. The voice of the weatherman's predictions for tomorrow's forecast was faintly heard. She had turned the volume down.

Relieved to be out of his clothes, he set his briefcase on the chair and slipped into bed. He snuggled against her, in some ways thankful that she was asleep. He was much too tired to give any thought to anything more than getting the sleep he'd been missing.

She stirred and whispered, "Hi."

Sixteen

"Hi, yourself," he responded as he gently kissed her shoulder, then relaxed his head on the soft pillow next to hers. "Miss me?"

"Just a little," Dominique replied. "Sure glad you're back. You can tell me about it in the morning."

Gale was more exhausted than he thought. It had been a rough journey, and now it was time to rest. Sleep came easily and quickly.

The next morning, as Dominique rolled to the side of the bed, stood, and walked to the shower, he couldn't take his eyes off her. She was graceful and lovely, and he had no longing to be anywhere but there. The aroma of shampoo pleased him. He found the remote and tuned into the news. The morning news reporter was on location in the nation's capitol as he filed his report.

"...the Pentagon announced today that shipping arms to Saudi allies is risky business, but sources close to the president say an extension of American defenses will likely be in the Middle East, in particular, the Saudi Peninsula, as well as possible areas friendly to American policy. Fear of similar Cuban missile situations such as..."

Gale's mind wandered back to his late friend, remembering his taking of sides with the president, and wondering what he could possibly do next. His gig with Bortens over, should he simply forget about it and go home?

"President Fenimore leaves today for the three Pacific Coast States of Washington, Oregon, and California. His reelection committee fears that the western states might cast their votes to the Democrat

candidate. Next stop, Portland, Oregon, where the Oregon Republican Committee will host a thousand-dollar-a-plate dinner in honor of President Fenimore..."

They walked in silence, hand in hand, to her apartment in the Village. This time, saying good-bye carried a sadness that he hadn't felt for a long time. There was something very special about her. They turned the corner to her apartment and stopped at the bottom of the steps. Not a word was spoken between them. Their touch said it all. Tightly, they held each other for only a few seconds, when she relaxed her hold, kissed his lips, and turned to climb the steps, pausing at the landing to see him one last time.

SEVENTEEN

The normal feelings of a job well done were absent. Something was missing, but Gale could not put his finger on it. He remembered feeling the same after leaving Judge Rickey's office. Maybe because he had not told the judge the entire story. But, in any event, he felt unsettled. Sure, he had gotten Bortens off the hook, but other names were dangling—Amacon, Fenimore, Cavalli, the hit man. He could easily write the whole thing off as someone else's problem. As he explored what possible effect it could have on him, he decided to follow his hunches once again.

He drove the rental car to within walking distance to the Capitol building's main entrance. A fake ID and a quick explanation to the guard that he was a treasury enforcement agent looking into Senator Brewer's death gained him not only entrance to the building but a key to the late senator's office. Luckily, nothing had been removed, not even the Brewer family photo that occupied a corner of the massive oak desk. Gale quickly got to work before the guard could realize that he'd been duped.

He searched the desk drawers, then began scanning through the credenza files. He didn't know exactly what he was looking for, but felt strongly that he'd recognize it once he saw it. There it was. A file folder with a single word written on the tab—"AMACON."

He swung around and placed the file folder on the late senator's desk, opened it, and began reading its handwritten contents.

AMACON—meeting with Allen Adams showed real possibilities: vice president, for sure; Can Cavalli pull it off? Probably not. Act alone? Probably. Must determine

"What's this all about?" Gale mumbled aloud. "What can't Cavalli pull off and why? Act alone? Who can act alone? And do what?"

Gale figured that the answers could only be in one place. The trick was to get inside Amacon Electric. He kept reading through the files, trying to find anything he could use— a clue that would help him infiltrate Amacon. There it was, staring him in the face.

Allen Adams hangs out at the Arlington Club. Ex-congressman from Oregon...

He rummaged through Brewer's business-card file until he found the perfect one. Just then he heard a slight tap on the door, followed by a key inserted into the lock. Before it opened, Gale grabbed the family photo, and had his hand on the doorknob as it opened.

"Thank you so much," Gale said as he brushed passed the guard. "Mrs. Brewer just wanted this photo," he said over his shoulder as he headed for the exit.

By the time he got to the Arlington Club, it was nearly happy hour. A stolen business card and a convincing explanation to the duty-host that he was a junior senator from Oregon here to have drinks with Allen Adams gained him entrance. The host pointed to Adams, who was sitting alone at a small table. Luckily the place was packed, and there was not an open table. Even the bar was jammed. Gale squeezed into the service area reserved for cocktail waitresses.

Gale asked the bartender for a Diet Coke served in a cocktail glass and to keep his tab open for both he and Mr. Adams over at that far table. "Oh, and by the way," Gale directed, "keep mine Diet Coke."

Banking that Adams had never socialized with, let alone ever met, any junior congressman from any state, Gale approached Adams with the card in his shirt pocket, should he need it.

"Good afternoon," Gale said as he placed the frosty glass of Diet Coke on the table. "Name's O'Malley, congressman from Oregon. Mind if I join you for a second while I'm waiting for an open tennis court?"

Startled, and with his mind in deep thought, Adams nodded and motioned for O'Malley to have a seat, which he did.

Gale thought about making small talk but figured that he would go for it. "You play much?"

"Huh?" Adams replied, his mind racing a million miles an hour. "Oh, you mean tennis? No, never touch it." Before Gale could respond, Adams asked, "What did you say you did?"

"Senator from Oregon." Gale continued, "Where do you work?"

"I'm in the background a lot," Adams replied. "Did you say Oregon?"

At this point, he was sure that Adams had taken the bait, but he also knew that he'd have to use caution as he pressed him further. "Yes sir. This is my first term in DC, and I'm sure looking forward to doing my part."

"A little gung-ho perhaps?" Adams quipped.

"I prefer the term 'enthusiastic,'" he smiled, eager to engage Adams in more light conversation, while taking advantage of his new drinking partner's eagerness to expound on his vast political experience. After all, Gale was a seasoned listener and a gifted persuader; plus he nearly always got what he wanted. He raised his glass to meet Adams's and almost simultaneously both men toasted the occasion, "Cheers."

"Let's have another," Adams demanded, as he held up a hand to signal the bartender. He turned his attention back to Gale, as a college professor about to begin a new lecture. "You've got a lot to learn about Washington, my man, a lot to learn."

"That's what I'm here for," Gale replied. Mentally, he discarded his earlier excuse of waiting for a tennis court; it had served its purpose as an opener, but now it was no longer necessary. Thank God for Brewer's business card file, he said to himself, then addressed Adams. "You're the teacher…and I am a ready and most willing learner. Thanks for the drink…cheers again!"

Adams returned the gesture and gave Gale a compliment. "You seem to have that killer instinct, my man, if you know what I mean. Some of us are working on a certain political agenda as we speak."

"I'm listening," Gale said. "What type of agenda?"

During the next two hours, Adams had a few more drinks to take his mind off his current problems, while Gale, drinking only Diet Coke, continued with his leading questions, steering the conversation in one direction. Finally, the conversation reached a point where Gale was certain that Adams actually believed that he was one of Adams's good old boys-in-training, and ready to fight for whatever causes Adams might have in mind.

Gale drank the rest of his drink, set it on the coaster, and looked Adams squarely in the eyes. "I think it's time you take me under your wing and give me a chance to prove myself. As a freshman, I'd do just about anything for the good of our country."

Adams extended his hand across the table, in agreement that what they were about to engage in would, indeed, be for the good of the country. He fetched a business card from his shirt pocket and handed it to Gale. "Be at that address tonight at eleven sharp."

Gale took the card and recognized the formal address of Amacon Electric. At least this time, he was invited. "I'm looking forward to it." He looked up and nodded at a non-existent tennis partner and faced Adams. "Looks like my court's ready. See you tonight."

* * * * * * *

Gale was sure that by now, Adams had ran a check on the name O'Malley. At least he hoped that was the case. Gale pulled into Amacon Electric's parking lot, but this time he entered through the front door. Two men were seated inside. He recognized Adams but not the other. As Adams and Gale shook hands, Adams introduced the other man. "Mr. O'Malley, may I present Mr. Dean Cavalli."

Gale shook Cavalli's hand, and it finally dawned on him that he had just shaken hands with the head of the CIA.

Cavalli spoke first. "Mr. Adams tells me you are eager to serve your country."

"That I am, Mr. Cavalli," Gale agreed, wondering if either of the two men would ever question him about his so-called job as a legislator, or checked him out.

"Good then, we need someone like you on our team," Cavalli continued.

"I'm happy to get involved," Gale said in a reassuring tone. "What can I do to help?"

"Mr. Adams also tells me that you are not at all pleased with the current situation. Of course, by that I mean the present administration."

"That is so true." Gale could not actually remember saying such, but since it suited the moment's purpose well, so be it.

"A large group of politicians are going to unseat the president," Cavalli explained. "Specifically, we're going to have him, ah, removed from office."

"By impeachment?" Gale asked, by then knowing for sure that he'd been checked out. Although somewhat plentiful on other continents, Mercenaries were a rare breed in Washington. He felt sure that his services would be needed somewhere along the line.

"By any means possible. Are you with us so far?"

"Absolutely." Gale said, hoping he sounded convincingly, waiting for the plot to thicken.

"You see, Mr. O'Malley, this will leave the vice president in charge, and it should be no shock to you to learn that he wouldn't stand a chance against the other party's candidate, agreed?"

"Oh yes," Gale agreed. "Not a chance."

"That's the plan in a nutshell, Mr. O'Malley. Once Fenimore is out of office, the VP takes over and, presto, the country is concerned about his ineptness and, presto again, our man is elected next fall."

Gale still had no clue how he would fit into all this, so he became abrupt. "Look," he said, "let's get right down to it. As far as I can see, an impeachment process is out of the question because there doesn't seem to be enough time. So, the only alternative I see is to simply get rid of him." He paused, then continued, "I'd be for that."

Adams gave Cavalli a nod and took over the conversation. "Tell me, Mr. O'Malley. Would you be interested in taking part in all this? Now think for a moment before giving us your answer. It's important, and you would be doing your country a service."

Gale figured that if anyone were listening in on this conversation, he'd be considered not only naive, but also stupid. Not only that, he'd probably be asked to shoot President Fenimore. With all that on his mind, he still agreed. "Count me in; but what part can I play?"

At this point, Gale just wanted answers, and he was willing to push the two men as far as he could to get them. He knew that he'd not see either again, so he planned on going along with anything they said.

"We have this problem," Adams said. "We have this certain, shall we say, contractor who has botched things up for us and, well, we would like you to ride herd on him."

"Ride herd?" Gale asked.

"Keep in touch with him," Cavalli said to clarify his last statement. "You see, we've lost a very important middleman and we'd like you to take his place, so to speak. Relay messages to our contractor…that sort of activity."

By this time, Gale's hunches were right on. Adams and Cavalli were referring to his late friend, Senator Brewer, as their middleman. The contractor? Not only did he know him, but he had a few scars and bruises to prove it. These two jokers were plotting to assassinate the president to make it easier for their candidate to become elected. They were certainly right about the vice president—no match for any party's candidate. That must have been what Senator Brewer meant by his notation. Then another sinking feeling overtook him. If these guys were responsible for all the deaths that he was aware of, how many others were there and, the biggest question of all, would he be next?

"So what's our next move?" Gale asked, hopefully with the appropriate body language to ensure he was one of them, and that he'd make it out of the meeting in one piece.

Cavalli and Adams stood simultaneously, one shaking Gale's hand, then the other. "Tomorrow night, same time and place. We'll have more details then." Adams directed.

"It seems as though you've changed your lifestyle a bit, Mr. O'Malley," Cavalli said, with enough smirk to let on that he had done his homework on the mercenary turned congressman.

By the time he reached his car, Gale was relieved to be outside of Amacon's office and away from the meeting with those two lunatics. He unbuttoned his shirt, and retrieved the tiny recorder that he had taped to his chest, and smiled. No way would a soldier of furtune with his background be frisked for a weapon, nor a recorder.

Again he thought of Senator Brewer. No wonder he was killed. Could it be that his late friend had plans of his own—maybe warn the president? He drove from Amacon's parking lot with no intention of making tomorrow's meeting because he had intentions of his own—track down and stop the assassination from taking place. Recalling the media announcements of President Fenimore's leaving for Portland today, Gale drove the rental car to the airport, where he dropped it off and bought a ticket to Portland.

EIGHTEEN

Bill Gale grabbed the first cab in line and instructed the driver to head toward downtown. Figuring that the downtown district, including the building where his office was located, would be secured by Secret Service and the Portland Police in anticipation of the president's arrival, he pointed toward the Lloyd Center exit, where he spotted a print shop in a small strip mall off Martin Luther King Boulevard.

He told the driver to wait at the curb, saying he would only be a minute. Using their computer, he accessed his own, bringing up a program he had designed to design ID badges, letters of recommendation, and official press passes, among other things. He chose the press pass file, entered his name as the CEO of Portland's *Oregonian* newspaper, and printed it on card stock, along with an ID saying the same. He then called the paper to verify that the CEO was in Europe for another week.

After crossing the Broadway Bridge, the cab pulled to the curb at Front Street, under the Burnside Bridge where, on the weekends, the area was filled with Saturday Market vendors and shoppers. He went the rest of the way on foot.

He spotted an *Oregonian* at the newsstand. Although a paperweight covered part of the front page, the headlines told the story of President Fenimore's appearance tomorrow night. The roadblocks and security force within a ten-block radius of the Benson Hotel confirmed that the president's arrival had already taken place.

Gale played his hunches. He did not know when, where, or how it would happen, but his gut told him it was a sure thing. The biggest question was would he recognize the man who had left him for dead?

He approached a mounted policeman, showed him the fresh press pass, and was granted admission to the sidewalk beyond the barricade that led him to the main entrance of the Benson Hotel. All that remained were the scores of Secret Service. Gale walked with an air that befitted a man of his title—the wealthy owner of the *Oregonian*, a very influential person in the community, but most important, the largest sponsor of tomorrow's dinner, a fact that Gale had picked up from the *Oregonian* a few minutes earlier.

A flash of his press pass and an officious nod gained him access to the hotel, where he had the run of the place, except maybe for the top floor on which the presidential suite was located.

* * * * * * * * * *

Eighteen

Jopaq sat at the bar at the top of the US Bank Tower with a cocktail on the table in front of him. He studied the direct line of vision from where he sat to the hotel. Even a better view, he calculated, would be from the two-story office building between them, which would have a front seat view of the Benson's main entrance on Broadway.

* * * * * * * * * *

Gale checked out the ballroom that had been prepared for the president's dinner party. Uniformed set-up crew scurried about, adorning the round tables with their finest china and their whitest linens. A banner welcoming President Fenimore hung tightly on the curtained wall behind the dignitary table. He spied a Secret Service agent barking orders to another. When the agent receiving the orders walked briskly away, Gale approached the other, press pass in hand, hoping it would do the trick and gain him access to the whole place

"Good day," Gale greeted, one arm outstretched and the other flashing the press pass. "May I speak with you in private?" If the agent bought it, he would be in for sure.

The agent removed his shades, nodded his agreement to Gale's relief, and gestured toward the row of chairs that filled one wall, probably for the press.

"I want to be perfectly sure that everything is set for tomorrow's dinner," Gale began, and without allowing the agent the time to question the stranger in front of him or raise the slightest doubt about his credentials, he continued. "You realize, of course, that I am the sponsor of the event, and I wanted you to know that I'll be on the premises from now until tomorrow's dinner, you know, just to satisfy myself." He paused again, while watching the agent's visual reaction, then continued, "I won't be in the way, and I hope that isn't an imposition. I've been cleared you know." Gale knew that he would compromise himself if he mentioned anything about an attempted assassination, so he kept it to himself for the time being.

Without hesitating, the agent replied, "I think we can oblige. I'm Agent Robinson, head of this particular detail." Robinson reached into his pocket and fetched a VIP badge, opened and closed the clasp to make sure it worked, then handed it to Gale. "This should do it, sir. If anyone questions you, have them radio me immediately." Having said that, militarily he stood, shook Gale's hand, and headed toward the hallway, leaving Gale alone in the ballroom.

* * * * * * * * * *

Jopaq slipped by the mounted policeman and entered the office building he had spotted from his perch at the bar. He took the elevator to the top floor, scanned all the offices, and then took the stairs to the next floor below, where he did the same. Finally on the third floor, he spotted the perfect office. The printing on the door read "Tom Welch, Engineer."

He quietly opened it and entered a suite of two offices, one behind the other. No one was in the front office, which was perfect. He retrieved his silenced weapon, held it behind him, and proceeded to the rear office.

A startled engineer looked up and said, "Yes, can I help you?"

Eighteen

The deadly Jopaq walked toward the window as if to look down at the street below. Before the startled engineer uttered a word, Jopaq raised the pistol and fired. The silent bullet ripped through the engineer's skull, forcing him and his chair to the carpet adjacent to the oak desk. Jopaq was right—a marvelously clear view of the Benson's main entrance. He locked the outer door, checked his watch, and waited.

* * * * * * * * * *

Gale tried to put himself in the mind-set of the assassin, as he scoured the massive room. A technician walked to the podium, tapped the microphone with a finger, and waited for a correction from the control room. Obviously pleased with the setting, he left the room. Gale followed, through a short hallway and up a double flight of stairs to a closed door that opened after the technician knocked. Gale put his hand on the door, stopping it from closing.

The technician that Gale had followed appeared to be a veteran at what he did for the hotel. His graying hair was closely cropped but just long enough to hide the wire earpieces of his frameless glasses. "Is there something we can do for you?" asked the somewhat startled technician.

"Yes, and sorry to startle you," Gale replied, revealing the press pass with a smile to set both men's minds at ease. "I'm just snooping around...hope you don't mind."

"Anything particular we can show you?" asked the younger man at the controls.

"Yes," Gale responded, as he placed his head near the spotlight that, when it was on, would shoot a steady beam of light to the podium. He sized up the opening as being about three feet square "Are there any other places—cubby holes if you will—that look down into the ballroom?"

Both men thought for a second; then the older technician answered. "Nope. This is it."

"I take it you would know," queried Gale.

"Yup. Been here over sixteen years," replied the older technician. "Handling the sound for all that time."

Confident in the technician's statements, Gale left the two men and returned to the ballroom, where he checked all entrances into and exits out of the massive room; every one of them had a Secret Service agent standing closely by. Confident that all was in order for the ballroom, he left the building, and walked around the entire block, searching for anything that might give him a clue as to where and when an assassination attempt might occur. There was an agent standing in every entry to every building on both sides of the street. From the looks of the outside area surrounding the hotel, Gale was again confident that adequate security was in place.

* * * * * * * * * *

After watching the security details surrounding the Benson, Jopaq had second thoughts about his present position. He picked up his things and left the room, more concerned about the time he had wasted than having taken the life of an innocent man. He closed the door behind him.

* * * * * * * * * *

Satisfied that everything was in order, Gale asked the front desk for a room, using the excuse that although he lived in the ritziest part of Portland, he would prefer staying in the hotel as a convenience to him. The clerk gladly granted his wish, and Gale hit the sack, but could not sleep.

His mind was on tomorrow's event. He fought with what he thought was the reality of the situation—tomorrow there would be an attempt on President Fenimore's life. But since he could not reveal his true identity, for fear of being escorted out of the place, he had to handle this one on his own. Sleep did not come easily, and the morning came sooner than he had wanted.

* * * * * * * * * *

A small, well-dressed man crossed Broadway, and walked up to a man in coveralls, bending into the open rear door of the van that was parked at the curb alongside the hotel's side door. To onlookers, the friendly confrontation appeared quite simply to be that of the boss playfully slapping his employee on the back—a simple greeting. What they did not see was the lethal dose of quick-acting poison from a well-hidden syringe. Jopaq pushed the dead electrician into the van, then followed, closing the door. The spare set of coveralls hanging on a hook fit him perfectly. He took the badge off the dead man's coveralls and pinned it on his own.

A half-block down, a cook on smoke break leaned against the open door, while another did the same against the brick wall, partially blocking the entrance to the kitchen's side door. Toolbox in hand, Jopaq closed the van door, and excused his way past the two cooks and through the kitchen, into the elevator that was normally reserved for the kitchen staff. Luckily, a piece of masking tape was stuck to the second-floor button, on which was scribbled "control room."

* * * * * * * * * *

Not wishing to take any time for breakfast, Gale grabbed a quick cup of coffee and headed, once again, for the ballroom. At least a dozen agents stood on each of the four sides of the room. While he was standing there, half in and half out of the doorway, several others purposefully walked the hallways. His VIP badge on his lapel, he walked the beautifully ornate staircase to the second floor. Reaching the control room, he knocked. At first, there was no answer, but then the younger technician opened the door.

"Oh, good morning, sir," he greeted, opening the door wider. "Please come in."

"Thank you, but I'm just checking to see if everything is ready," Gale replied.

"We're shipshape sir," the technician said with confidence. "Everything is a go."

Gale believed the young man but issued a warning. "Please keep this door locked and don't let anyone in. I assume you have a code of some kind?"

"If you mean for the door, yes, we do," answered the technician. "Around noon or so, we'll begin using it. Five knocks, followed by two."

Gale gave him a thumbs-up and left. Before he did, though, he looked left down one corridor then right, down the other. Satisfied that everything was in order, he returned to the stairs and descended to the main floor.

* * * * * * * * * *

From his position, flat against the wall of the darkened hallway, Jopaq recognized him once again, and smiled, saying to himself, "Once again we meet; but this time you shall not get in my way." The deadly assassin moved quietly toward the control room door, on which he first tapped five times, followed by another two. No sooner had the young technician opened the door, than he was dead where he stood, shot squarely and silently between his eyes.

* * * * * * * * * *

It was around noon when they all arrived at the sidewalk in front of the Benson's main entrance. One by one, reporters passed through the tight security until everyone was admitted into the ballroom, where they were given instructions to their reserved seats and an itinerary printed on a half-sheet of paper.

Surprised at the early time of the day, Gale approached one of the agents. "Has there been a change for today's event?"

The Secret Service agent started to answer but covered his earpiece with one hand while holding the other up to signal that he could not speak at the moment. Then he relaxed both hands and replied. "Yes sir. The president will speak in one hour."

"An hour?" Gale questioned. "But I thought—"

"The time has changed sir," the agent interrupted, apparently eager to end the conversation. "It is now a luncheon meeting."

It took Gale only a split second to realize that it was no doubt a luncheon meeting all along, and that publicity for a dinner meeting was simply that—publicity. He recognized too that everything that could be done was done. But the hunch welling deep within him would not subside.

Guests began arriving and entered through the same security system, until every seat in the ballroom was filled, including those reserved for the press, but not including the head table, which remained empty for a minute or so. Finally every chair was filled. Gale couldn't help but notice that not a single person was standing, except now him.

As waiters and waitresses brought out the food, Gale kept looking for something…anything unusual. He thought about rechecking the control room, but was convinced that the two technicians had it under control.

Someone from the head table, Gale didn't recognize him, walked to the podium, welcomed the attendees, apologized for the inconvenience of the last-minute time change, and followed by saying, "It would appear that all of you received the phone call. Thank you once again."

At this juncture, Gale lost interest in what was going on, so long as the president had yet to be introduced. His mind was racing as it flashed back to the incidents involving the hit man. Then it was time.

The next speaker, the governor of Oregon, introduced the president of the United States. As the crowd stood, showing their overwhelming support with a huge round of applause, President Fenimore entered from the right, shaking hands with all guests at that side of the head table, finally greeting the governor with a smart hug and a couple of pats on the back. Centered between a United States flag and one for Oregon, the president bid everyone to please sit, thanking everyone for taking time from their schedules.

He greeted all the ladies and gentlemen and honored guests, and spoke softly but firmly about what must have been hot subjects, but those that Gale had no desire to hear at this particular time.

Gale rose from his seat and approached an agent, more for the opportunity to watch the president from another angle. Then, there it was—a spark from a point im-mediately in front of the podium. "Did you see that?" he said to the agent, knowing the spark could not have been the result of a bullet—not with the hit man's accuracy.

Before the agent had a chance to respond, Gale dashed toward the podium to a point where he saw the spark. Immediately, several agents followed in an attempt to stop this mad man whom they instinctively felt was a would-be assassin. Gale reached the point at which a black cord ran from a receptacle in front of the podium to the microphone that the president was about to touch to make a point. He broke away from one agent's grip, and dove for it. As he snapped the cord from the receptacle, a bright electrical spark knocked him to the floor.

In the few seconds it took for him to recover from the near-death electrical shock, the remaining agents had escorted the president from the premises. The one who had nearly stopped Gale helped him up and asked if he could call a medic.

Gale was in high gear, now focusing on the dark hallway upstairs. He knew something was wrong and it had to do with electric power. He motioned for the agent to follow him as he ran toward the steps.

The control room door was ajar. Gale pushed it open and there they were—two technicians on the floor in their own pools of blood. The agent walked to the control panel, but Gale grabbed his arm and stopped him.

"Wait!" Gale warned. "Don't touch anything." He noticed a heavy wire running from an electrical outlet to a black box that appeared to be out of place. A second wire ran from the box to a metal post sticking out of the bottom of the control panel. He took a spoon from a coffee cup and threw it onto the control panel. The force from the resultant spark and bang flipped the spoon into the air, where it seemed to hang in suspension, then fall to the floor, half of it gone. Gale thought, What an ingenious attempt to kill the president—one touch of the microphone and that would have been it! Then it hit him. The would-be assassin left the control panel hot-wired for a reason. This was an attempted double hit—first the president, then himself. He felt a little pleased that he had foiled another attempt by his nameless foe.

Gale left the Secret Service agent to take care of things there, and went back to the ballroom, expecting to find someone from the president's entourage, but not a single government employee remained.

Eighteen

At this point, he wasn't sure what to do. He had handled the Bortens incident plus, on his own, had saved the president. Figuring his time here was done, he headed for the exit, only to be stopped by the same agent from the upstairs control room.

"Excuse me sir," the agent said. "May we talk?"

"By all means," Gale replied.

"Sir, the president wishes to speak to you...in private, of course," said the agent. Without allowing time for a response, he continued. "Please follow me."

The agent led Gale down a flight of steps to the lower level, past a dozen or more agents, and into the hotel's wine storage area. President Fenimore appeared no more shaken than as if nothing had happened. The group of agents allowed Gale through to where the president extended his hand. "I don't know who you are or where you came from, but I owe you my life. Please accept my deepest and most heartfelt thanks."

Gale took the president's firm grip. "The name's Gale, Mr. President," he began, thinking it wouldn't hurt to give his real name in this circumstance. But he still did not wish to let on his real identity or his purpose for being there. "I'm a freelance writer here to cover your speech."

"How did you know—"

"A lucky guess, Mr. President," he interrupted. "I noticed the sparks from the microphone cord and it just didn't seem right. Nothing more." Gale wanted out of there before the Secret Service decided to make a file on him.

President Fenimore again shook Gale's hand, while saying, "If there is ever anything I can do for you, please don't hesitate."

"I'll remember your kind invitation, Mr. President," Gale said. "I'm going to reach into my pocket for a tape recorder, so don't everyone jump me, okay?" He withdrew the tiny tape recorder from his pocket and handed it to President Fenimore. "I think you'll find this interesting, sir!"

He made his way the few blocks to his own office, where he threw himself into one of the leather chairs, let out a deep sigh, and smiled about the tape. He wished he could be there when the president played the tape, which had more than enough evidence to put Cavalli and Adams away for life, as well as close down the Amacon operation for good. He knew that the president would not take their acts of treason very lightly.

He thought, too, about all that had occurred over the past few days. He came to the conclusion that the president was correct in his assessment of America's position with the Middle East. He felt discouraged, though, that such disagreements existed between the higher-ups in government, and wondered if it was simply a power struggle. It made sense that career CIA leaders were frustrated with changing policies with every change in administration. He reflected on his own short career there, knowing that it was common knowledge that the intelligence community knew more than everyone else, no matter the cost. He also knew that intelligence matters cannot change with the tide of new administration. Consistency had to be the best choice, or so he thought at the moment. Rather than try to second-guess the entire thing, Gale thought it best to turn his attentions to things that he could control, that is, other than the tape recording that was now in good hands. Right now, the only thing he could control was his thirst for a cold beer.

* * * * * * * * * *

The Frankfurt airport was busy with seasonal travelers. The conveyer started with a hum, bringing pieces of luggage from the recently arrived Lufthansa flight. First a few pieces, then a bunch of them together. For the most part, the crowd was mingling a few feet away from the conveyer. As more luggage came down the line, a few stepped up to claim theirs, grabbing one at a time, then scurrying off to complete their journey.

A short man, dressed in a smart blazer, supported himself on a black cane with a brass handle and rubber tip. Suffering from an apparent leg injury, he limped through the crowd, his eyes searching for a single bag. Spotting a soft-sided one, he gently lifted it and placed it on the floor in front of him. He quickly examined the bag for outward signs of damage, then switched his attention to its contents. He removed the small padlock and unzipped one of the two side pockets that ran the length of the case. Gently, he inserted two fingers, searching for two black nylon tubes. He pulled one partially out, then replaced it. He put his arm full length into the pocket and slid it down the tubes, delicately feeling for possible breaks.

Everything was intact. If there had been any breakage, he doubted very much if he'd be seeking a settlement with the airlines. Although he had no way of knowing if his mission had succeeded, his Cayman Island bank account was richer by a few hundred thousand, more than enough to buy the airline.

THE END

ACKNOWLEDGMENTS

I thank Jason Davis, my editor, for his kind devotion to this project and his empathy in dealing with me, a first-time published author. I also thank American Book Publishing for taking a chance on me.

I thank Alan H. Crowe, one of the highest regarded legal investigator and process server in the country, who had the faith in me to present me with my first undercover, corporate espionage assignment.

I thank Carolyn Latteier who, by her own award-winning writings, inspired me to put it all down on paper.

ABOUT THE AUTHOR

He seems like an ordinary guy—house in the suburbs, two cars, he volunteers at the kids' swim meets, plays golf on Sunday. But unknown to his friends and associates, he leads a double life as a spook in the secret world of corporate espionage.

With modest beginnings as a deputy sheriff in the not-so-wild West, Klausman longed for more danger in his life. This led him to the CIA, where he quickly learned that allowing his destiny to be controlled by others didn't match his lifestyle.

How he ended up in the business intelligence community is as guarded as the tasks he performs. His secret identity allows his huge corporate clients to keep a certain amount of deniability. Why? His methods may not survive close scrutiny in some circles.